A ROYAL VOW
OF CONVENIENCE

A ROYAL VOW OF CONVENIENCE

BY

SHARON KENDRICK

* * *

'Sharon Kendrick is such a talented author
and a good friend. Her books are all-consuming,
and I race through the pages from start to finish
every time I pick one up.'
—LYNNE GRAHAM

MILLS
BOON

First published in Great Britain 2016
By Mills & Boon, an imprint of HarperCollins*Publishers*
1 London Bridge Street, London, SE1 9GF

Large Print edition 2017

© 2016 Sharon Kendrick

ISBN: 978-0-263-07080-4

Printed and bound in Great Britain
by CPI Antony Rowe, Chippenham, Wiltshire

This book is dedicated to
my two greatest achievements—
Celia Campbell & Patrick Kendrick,
who are talented, hard-working and funny.
I'm very proud to be your mum.

CHAPTER ONE

THE CLATTER WAS deafening as the helicopter descended from a cloudless blue sky, and a nervous bead of sweat trickled down between Sophie's breasts.

'He's here,' said Andy abruptly as the blades stopped turning. 'Don't look so worried, Sophie. Rafe Carter might be the big boss but he doesn't bite. He just doesn't suffer fools gladly and as long as you remember that, you'll be okay. Okay?'

'Okay,' Sophie echoed dutifully. But her throat was still tight with tension as Andy left the veranda and ran towards the helicopter where a powerfully built man had just appeared at the open door, raking his fingers through dark and wind-ruffled hair. Pausing briefly to scan the horizon, he shook his head as a busty blonde in a tight blue uniform tried to get his attention, before jumping to the dusty ground, leaving the woman staring after him—her shoulders hunched with dejection.

Another feeling of panic prickled over Sophie's skin but now it was underpinned with something else. Something which made her pulse start racing as the man stood very still, just staring at the land—his frozen stance drawing attention to his proud profile and the shadowed jut of his jaw.

Even from this distance she could see the hard definition of his body. In an immaculate suit, which hugged his muscular physique, he looked sophisticated and urbane—as out of place in the dusty Outback setting as his expensive helicopter. Everything about him proclaimed the fact that this was the billionaire owner of one of the world's biggest telecommunications companies, whose enormous cattle station was simply one of his 'hobbies'. Rafe Carter. Even the name sounded sexy. She'd overheard the other staff talking about him—tantalising snatches of gossip which had made her ears prick up—though she'd been careful not to pry or show her curiosity.

Because Sophie had learnt very quickly that if she wanted to keep her identity secret, it was better to be seen and not heard. To dress demurely and fade into the background. To not ask questions about the man who owned this property and all the land as far as the eye could see. All she knew was that he was rich. Very rich. That he liked planes and art and beautiful women—in addition to a rural Australian life he dipped in and out of as he pleased. Her breasts prickled with an unfamiliar beat of anticipation. She just hadn't expected him to be quite so...*mesmerising.*

She watched as Andy moved forward and the two men exchanged a few words of greeting before walking towards the homestead as the helicopter rose back up into the sky. It was hot on the veranda. Even at this early hour the mercury was shooting up the scale. Summer had arrived and sometimes it felt as if she were living in a giant sauna. Her palms were covered in a fine layer of sweat and she rubbed them over her cotton shorts, willing her heart to stop pounding—because surely that would make her unease seem somehow *obvious*.

She wondered what it was about the arrival of Rafe Carter which made her feel as if her world were about to come tumbling down around her. Fear she would be found out? That he might succeed where everyone else on this cattle station had failed—and work out who she really was? That he would discover the crazy lengths she'd gone to in order to secure herself a place here in the wild peace of the Australian Outback, because she'd wanted to escape from her gilded life and forge a more worthwhile existence? She'd never met him, but it wasn't beyond the realms of possibility that he'd seen her photograph in a newspaper—because didn't their gilded worlds have distant connections? Her mind began to race even faster. And what if he *did* find out—then what?

A series of disturbing scenarios flashed before her and she clenched her fists as a wave of determination swept over her. Because that wasn't going to happen. She wouldn't let it. For the first time in her life she'd been enjoying the simple pleasures of anonymity and the rewards of honest hard work and was feeling cautiously optimistic about the future. Nobody knew who she was and nobody cared. There were no eyes following her every move. She was on her own—properly on her own—and it was both daunting and exciting. It couldn't last. She knew that. Her brother had given her an ultimatum and time was fast running out. He wanted her back in Isolaverde—preferably by Christmas, but certainly by the time of her little sister's nineteenth birthday at the end of February. In a couple of months it would all be over and she was going to miss the sense of peace and freedom she'd known in this out-of-the-way place. She was going to have to return to the world she'd run away from and face up to the future, but she wanted to do it on her own terms. To leave here in the same way she'd arrived—without fuss or fanfare.

Leaving the heat which hung over the veranda

like a heavy blanket, Sophie hurried into the kitchen where the air-conditioning did little to cool her heated skin. She fanned her face with her hand as she heard the heavy tread of masculine footfall and tried not to let her nerves get the better of her.

'Sophie? Come and meet the boss.'

Andy's broad Australian accent shattered her thoughts and suddenly it was too late for any more reflection because the station manager was walking into the kitchen, a smile wreathing his face—in stark contrast to the expression of the man who followed him. And try as she might, Sophie still couldn't tear her eyes away from the newcomer, even though her upbringing had taught her it was rude to stare.

Close up, he was even more spectacular. His hard-boned face was shockingly beautiful and so was his body. But his physical perfection was underpinned by a dark quality which shimmered around him like an aura—an edge of danger which was making her feel self-conscious. Did he know the effect he had on women? she wondered. Did he realise that her mouth was as dry as the dust in the yard outside and that her breasts had started to swell, so that they were pushing against the suddenly constricting material of her cheap underwear? She wondered how he managed to look so cool in a suit and, as if reading her thoughts, he slid the jacket from his broad shoulders so she was confronted by the hint of hard, honed torso—shadowy beneath the pristine silk of his white shirt.

Another bead of sweat trickled down her cleavage and soaked into her T-shirt as she met the steely grey eyes which were trained in her direction. He narrowed them in contemplation as he looked her up and down and Sophie's apprehension gave way to indignation because she wasn't used to men looking at her that way. Nobody *ever* stared at her so openly. As if he had every right to do so. She swallowed. As if he knew exactly what she was thinking about him and his beautiful face and body...

'Rafe.' Andy's voice was relaxed as he gestured in her direction. 'This is Sophie—the woman I was telling you about. She's been cooking for us for nearly six months now.'

'Sophie...?'

It was the first word he'd spoken—a lash of dark silk which whipped through the air towards her. Rafe Carter raised his eyebrows in question and Sophie gave a nervous smile in response. She knew she shouldn't hesitate because hesitation was dangerous. Just as she knew she should have had this answer all pat and ready—and she would have done if she hadn't been so distracted by the lure of his deep, mellifluous voice and the effect that paralysing stare was having on her.

'It's Doukas. Sophie Doukas,' she said, using the surname of her Greek grandmother, knowing that nobody would be able to contradict her, because she hadn't shown anyone her papers. A wave of guilt washed over her. She'd managed to distract them for long enough to forget they'd never seen them.

The steely gaze became even more piercing. 'Unusual name,' he observed.

'Yes.' Desperate to change the subject, she

cleared her throat, mustering up a smile from somewhere. 'You must be thirsty after your flight. Would you like some tea, Mr Carter?'

'I thought you'd never ask,' he drawled. 'And it's Rafe.'

'Rafe,' she repeated, aware that his cool tone contained the hint of a reprimand. *So pull yourself together. Start remembering that he's the boss and you're supposed to be pleasant and obedient.* 'Right.' She forced a smile. 'I'll make some right away. Andy, how about you?'

'Not for me, thanks.' The station manager shook his head. 'I'll wait for the morning smoko. See you outside when you've had a brew, Rafe. Take you on a quick tour.'

Sophie's self-consciousness spiralled as Andy walked out, leaving her alone with Rafe Carter in a room whose walls seemed to be closing in on her. And even though making tea was a task she performed countless times every day, she felt like a coiled spring as she busied herself around the kitchen, aware of his eyes following her every movement. His grey gaze seemed to laser through her as she lifted a kettle which suddenly felt ridiculously heavy. *Why was he even here?* she thought as she poured boiling water into the teapot. Andy had said he wasn't expected until springtime—by which time she would be gone and nothing but a distant memory. He certainly wasn't expected this close to Christmas—which was now only weeks away.

She took a cup down from the dresser. It had been easy to forget Christmas in this exotic and tropical area of Australia, with its lush foliage and steamy heat, and the kind of birds and mammals which she'd only ever seen in nature documentaries. Yet because the men had demanded it, she'd made a stab at decorating the homestead with paper chains and plastic holly and a cheap tree made out of tinsel which she'd bought from the local store. The effect had been garish but it was so *different* that it had allowed her to forget all the things she was used to.

But now the familiar images of what she'd left behind came crowding into her mind, as she thought about Christmas on her island home of Isolaverde. She pictured mulled wine and golden platters piled high with sugary treats. She thought about the enormous tree which took pride of place in the palace throne room, which was decorated with real candles and diligently lit by the legions of faithful staff who served her. And beneath it the huge pile of presents, which she and her brother would hand out every year to the children of the city. She remembered the eager looks lighting up their little faces and, without warning, a wave of loneliness came washing over her. Suddenly she felt *vulnerable*. She knew how easy it would be to just throw the towel in and go home, but she didn't want to do that. Not yet. Not until she'd worked out what she wanted her new future to be…

Giving the teapot a quick stir, she hoped Rafe would take his tea outside, or go to his own lavish quarters, which were in a separate part of this giant homestead. But her heart sank as he rested his narrow hips against the window sill with the look of a man who wasn't going anywhere. And, unlike most people, he seemed content to let the silence grow. Didn't he realise she was getting more flustered by the moment despite the fact that she'd spent her whole life being stared at? It just didn't usually affect her like this. It didn't make her breasts tingle, or a slug of disconcerting heat begin to gather low in her belly...

So say something. Pretend he's one of those countless strangers you've spent your life meeting and exchanging polite words with.

'Have you flown in from England today?' she questioned, pouring milk into a china jug.

He didn't smile back. 'No. I've been on an extended trip to the Far East and I arrived in Brisbane yesterday. I was so close that it seemed crazy not to visit.' His grey eyes gleamed. 'And just for the record, I don't live in England.'

She met the steely gaze. 'But I thought—'

'That my accent was English?'

She gave a weak smile. 'Well, yes.'

'They say you never really lose the accent you were born with, but I haven't lived there in a long time. Years, in fact.' He frowned. 'And speaking of accents—I can't quite work yours out. I don't think I've ever heard anything like it before. Are you Greek?'

Sophie distracted him by holding up the jug, her bright tone matching her smile. 'Milk? Sugar?'

'Neither, thanks. I'll take it how it comes.'

She handed him the tea, wishing he wouldn't stretch out his legs like that—a movement which was making the dark material of his trousers spread tautly over his powerful thighs. Was it his intention to get her gaze to linger there, like some reluctant voyeur? Yet ogling men was something she didn't do. It wasn't in her nature to be predatory. Any such behaviour would have been picked up and frowned on by the cameras which had followed her every move since birth. Even the man to whom she'd been betrothed—a man popularly known as one of the world's sexiest men—had never aroused this kind of heart-pumping interest, which was making her fingers start to tremble.

In an attempt to hide her nerves, she brushed

some imaginary crumbs from the table. 'So where *do* you live?' she questioned.

'Mainly in New York, although I lived here full-time when I first bought the station. But I move around a lot between cities—constantly on the move. I'm what you might call an urban gypsy, Sophie.' He took a sip of his tea, mocking eyes studying her over the rim of his cup. 'And you still haven't answered my question.'

'I'm sorry?' She batted him a confused look, hoping he might have forgotten. 'What question was that?'

'I asked if you were Greek.'

Sophie didn't want to lie but if she told him the truth it would be like hurling a bomb into the room. Her anonymity would be over and her sanctuary would end. There would be questions. Lots of them. Because what could she say?

I'm a princess who doesn't want to be a princess any more. I'm a woman who's been brought up in a palace who has never had to cope with real life before. A woman who has been hurt and humiliated. Who has struck out to discover if she can cope with life without the protection she's known all her life.

She met the cold gleam of his gaze. 'My grandmother was Greek,' she said. 'And Greek is my mother tongue.'

He was even more watchful now. 'Any other languages?'

'English. Obviously.'

'Obviously.' His eyes glinted. 'And that's the lot?'

She licked her bottom lip. 'I can get by in Italian. French, too.'

'Well now, aren't you the clever one?' he questioned softly. 'You certainly have a lot of qualifications for someone who's spent the last few months frying steak and buttering bread for a bunch of station workers.'

'I didn't realise linguistic ability was a bar to being a cook on a cattle station, Mr Carter.'

Their gazes clashed and Rafe tried not to be affected by the sudden challenge sparking from her eyes, which was easily as distracting as the pert thrust of her breasts. On one level he was aware she was playing games with him by avoiding his questions and he wasn't sure why. He frowned. But there was a lot he wasn't sure about right now. Plenty of young women came from abroad to work in remote parts of this country—but he'd never come across anyone like Sophie Doukas before. He wondered just what she was doing here, when she looked as out of place as a diamond you might find in the rough. Andy had told him that when she'd first arrived she'd been green and naïve, but had been eager to learn. Rafe had wondered why his gruff Australian station manager had employed someone without even the most basic of skills, but now he'd seen her—he had a pretty good idea why.

His throat grew dry.

Because she was beautiful.

Really beautiful.

Not the kind of beauty which came from spending hours in front of the mirror or having a plastic surgeon on speed-dial. Something told him she looked that way without even trying. Her cheekbones were high, her eyes as blue as a

Queensland sky and her dark hair was tied back in a shiny ponytail. She wore no make-up—but with lashes that long, he guessed she didn't need to. And her lips. Oh, man. Those lips. His groin hardened. Just one glance at them and he could think of a million different X-rated ways he'd like her to use them—starting with that cute pink tongue working a very fundamental kind of magic.

But her appeal didn't stop at her face. She had one of those bodies which looked amazing in clothes but probably better out of them. Even her cheap white T-shirt and unremarkable cotton shorts failed to disguise her long legs and curvy bottom, and she moved with the natural grace of a dancer. She was one very desirable female, that was for sure—and Rafe imagined Andy's reaction when he had first seen her. What man could have resisted a woman who looked like this, turning up out of the blue as if in answer to every hot-blooded man's dreams?

But Andy had also told him that she'd kept her distance. She wasn't one of those foreign backpackers keen to enjoy anything new—including sex. Apparently she hadn't flirted with the men or indicated that she might be up for some late-night hook-up. His manager had told him she seemed *wary* and could turn the ice on without really trying, which was why nobody had dared to make a pass at her. Rafe frowned. Yes. Wary was right. She was regarding him now in a way which reminded him of a bowerbird which had once flown into the homestead by mistake—its beautiful wings battering uselessly against the window pane as it tried to escape from its domestic confinement.

He took another sip of his tea, his interest stirred in more ways than one because he could sense she was trying to distance herself from him, and that never usually happened. He was used to instant compliance from the opposite sex whenever he wanted it. A gushing desire to tell him everything he ever wanted to know—and then more.

But not from Sophie Doukas it seemed. He wondered why she was being so cagey. And whether her reluctance to talk was responsible for the powerful beat of desire which was pooling even harder in his groin.

'No,' he conceded dryly. 'Your linguistic ability is to be commended, even if you haven't had much chance to practise your language skills out here in the bush.' He shifted his weight a little. 'I understand you and I are going to be sharing accommodation.'

She looked uncomfortable. 'We don't have to. I've been living in the far end of the main house since I arrived. Andy said it seemed crazy for it to stay empty and that it was much cooler in here. But now you're back...'

She looked him straight in the eyes without any hint of the flirtation he would have expected from any other woman in the circumstances.

'I can easily move into one of the smaller properties,' she continued stiffly. 'I'd hate to feel I was in your way.'

Rafe almost smiled. No. She definitely *wasn't* flirting. Hell. When had been the last time that had happened? 'That won't be necessary,' he

said. 'It's plenty big enough for two people.
I'm sure we won't have any problem keeping
out of each other's way. And I'm only passing
through—one night max. Which reminds me.'
He leaned back against the window and looked
at her speculatively. 'I don't remember Andy
mentioning how long you're planning on staying?'

He watched as her body language changed.
And how. She picked up a teaspoon she'd left
lying on the table and carried it over to the sink
as if it would explode if she didn't quickly plunge
it into a bowl of water.

'I…hadn't really decided,' she said, still with
her tensed back to him. 'Soon. Just after Christmas, probably.'

'But won't your family miss you at Christmas?' he probed. 'Or maybe you don't celebrate
Christmas?'

She turned to face him then and Rafe saw that
her face had grown pale. Her blue eyes had darkened so that suddenly she looked almost *fragile*
and he felt an unexpected kick of guilt—as if

he'd done something wrong. Until he reminded himself that all he'd done was ask her a straightforward question and, as the man who was paying her wages, he had every right to do that.

'Yes, I celebrate it,' she said quietly. 'But my parents are dead.'

'I'm sorry.'

She inclined her head. 'Thank you.'

'You don't have brothers, or sisters?'

Sophie thought how persistent he was—and how she wasn't used to being interrogated like this. Because nobody would usually *dare*. She wondered why he was so interested. Did he realise that his station manager had been less than meticulous when he'd interviewed her—or was there something else? She stared at the teapot and watched it blur in and out of focus. She was innocent, yes—but she wasn't completely stupid. She'd seen the look he'd given her when he walked into the kitchen—a look of surprise which had swiftly turned to one of appreciation. She had been subjected to a brief but very thorough evaluation of her face and her body—one she doubted he would have done if he'd known who she really was. But he didn't know, did he? And he wasn't going to find out.

Because her first instincts had been the right ones, as instincts so often were. She'd felt apprehension when she'd first seen him and she hadn't known why. But now she did. As he'd looked at her, she'd felt something alien. A feeling which had nothing to do with the fear of being found out, but which was just as disturbing. A sudden heaviness in her breasts and a melting sensation low in her belly. Her skin suddenly felt as if it were too tight for her body and her cheap underwear seemed to be digging into her flesh.

And just as she would have recognised sunburn if she'd never experienced it before, she knew that what she was feeling for Rafe Carter was desire. Hot and very real desire, which was making her heart pound so erratically. Making her wonder what it would be like to be held by Rafe Carter and have him touch her. For him to run those long olive fingers over her newly sensitised skin and take away some of this terrible aching. And she'd never felt that before, not with anyone.

Guilt rippled over her.

Not even with Luciano.

She realised he was still waiting for an answer and she struggled to extract some coherent answers from the unfamiliar erotic fog of her thoughts. 'I have a younger sister and a brother.'

'And won't they be expecting you home?'

Sophie shook her head. After she'd left Isolaverde, she had phoned to let her brother, Myron, know she was safe and well—and begged him not to send out any search parties. She'd told him she needed to escape the pressure of what had happened, and so far he had heeded her request. On the few occasions she'd managed to get online and search the news outlets, there had been no public acknowledgements regarding her sudden disappearance and her younger sister, Mary-Belle, had stepped in to take over all her official engagements. Maybe Myron understood that her pride had been hurt and she'd needed to get away to lick her wounds after her very public rejection by the man she'd been meant to marry. That she was more than happy to resume all the responsibilities of her role as princess, she just wanted a little time to get her head together. Or maybe he was just too busy ruling their island kingdom to pay her much attention. He took his position as King of Isolaverde very seriously and for too long now had been coming under pressure to find himself a suitable bride.

'You've got exactly six months to have your little stab at rebellion,' he had clipped out, over the crackly phone line. 'And if you're not back by February, then I will send out search parties to bring you home again. Make no mistake about that, Sophie.'

Remembering her brother's sense of control—and the way that people had always tried to control her all her life—Sophie turned round to meet Rafe Carter's inquisitive stare, knowing she had to stop him doing the same. So be strong. Ask *him* something, she thought. Put *him* on the spot.

'And how about *your* Christmas? You'll be

sitting around the Christmas tree with your own family, will you?' she questioned. 'Pulling crackers and singing carols in the old traditional way?'

His face hardened and Sophie saw something in the depths of his eyes which looked almost like pain. She blinked. Surely not. She couldn't imagine a powerful man like this ever *hurting*.

'That kind of Christmas only exists in fairy tales,' he said and suddenly his voice grew harsh with cynicism. 'And I never did believe in fairy tales.'

Abruptly he stood up and moved away from the window and suddenly he was close enough for Sophie to touch. Close enough for her to notice that his jaw was dark with the hint of new growth, even though he could barely have been out of bed for more than a few hours. As a symbol of virility, he couldn't have sent out a more potent message and another rush of unfamiliar desire pulsed through her.

'Why look,' he observed, his steely eyes glittering before they were shaded by his ebony lashes as he glanced down at her fingers. 'Your hands are trembling. What's the matter, Sophie? Is something bothering you?'

She suspected he knew exactly what was bothering her but she concealed her embarrassment behind a shake of her head.

'Actually, there is,' she said. 'I get nervous if someone stands around watching while I work—especially if that someone happens to be the boss. I'm about to start making the men their mid-morning smoko and you know how hungry they get.' She gave a quick smile, hoping it hid the way she was feeling. Hoping he wouldn't notice the fact that her nipples were pushing like little hard stones against her T-shirt or that her cheeks were getting hotter by the second. 'So if you'll excuse me?'

'I get the distinct feeling I'm being dismissed,' he said silkily. 'Which is something of a first. Still, since dedication to work is a quality I've always admired, you won't find me objecting.'

But before he reached the door he paused, and suddenly he was no longer the mildly curious boss asking idle questions about her background or pointing out that her fingers were trembling. Suddenly he was the billionaire station owner with the shiny helicopter, who was regarding her with a certain sense of entitlement.

'I have no objection to sharing the homestead with you, just as long as you realise that I like my own company. So please don't feel you have to seek me out or engage me in conversation, especially if I'm working. If it happens to be a beautiful day, we'll take that as a given, shall we?' His voice hardened. 'I certainly don't need to hear your views on the sunshine levels or hav- ing you brightly enquire how I'm planning to spend my day. Understand?'

Sophie met his piercing grey gaze, thinking that was possibly the rudest thing anyone had ever said to her. Engage him in conversation? Why, she'd rather talk to one of the large bugs which regularly scuttled across the veranda each morning! But her face betrayed nothing as she nodded, even if her voice was stiff. 'Of course.'

She was glad when the door swung shut behind

him. He was the most arrogant man she'd ever met—even more arrogant than her brother—but he was also the most attractive. By a mile. Briefly she closed her eyes as she reminded herself of the effect he'd had on her. She'd been stumbling and uptight in his company and that wasn't her. Just as trembling fingers and aching breasts weren't her either. She'd let him *get* to her just because he looked like some fallen Greek god who'd been given more than his fair share of sex appeal and she mustn't allow that to happen again. He was her boss—nothing more. A man who was just passing through.

But despite her best intentions, something made her go to the window as he crossed the yard and something kept her there, watching him.

The morning sun was touching his ebony hair with splashes of dark red and she could see the powerful thrust of his thighs as he walked. A pulse started beating deep in her groin and Sophie felt a yearning so powerful that she had to grip onto the window sill for support.

It was just unfortunate that Rafe Carter chose that very moment to turn around and catch her staring.

And she couldn't mistake the lazy arrogance of his smile.

CHAPTER TWO

IT WAS TORTURE having your boss hanging around for longer than he was supposed to. Sophie gave the bowl of cake mix a vicious stir as he began to walk across the yard towards her. Sheer torture. Why was he still here four days after telling her he was just 'passing through'? Wasn't he supposed to be some important international CEO with loads of calls on his time? Not someone who helped his men repair fences and muster cattle before standing in the evening sunlight with a bottle of cold beer held to his lips. Sophie swallowed. And why the hell did he have to walk around the place looking like...*that*?

Her heart pounded as she watched him approach the homestead, the expensive grey suit he'd worn on his arrival now just a memory. He was wearing faded denim jeans, which might as well have been *sprayed* onto his muscular legs, and a clinging black T-shirt, which emphasised his washboard abs and the powerful lines of his arms and shoulders.

It was getting uncomfortable. Embarrassing, even. Every time he came into her eye-line, a load of unsettling things started to happen to her body. Things which centred around her aching breasts and a newly sensitive spot between her thighs. Things which had never happened to her before. She'd tried telling herself that it was because she was in this very elemental place instead of the rarefied atmosphere of her palatial home which was making her so aware of her own physicality. She'd tried keeping out of his way as much as possible—scuttling out of sight whenever she spotted him in the distance—but nothing seemed to help. Whatever qualities Rafe Carter had, he had them in abundance and she just couldn't stop thinking about him…

He pushed open the door and walked into the air-conditioned cool of the kitchen. His black hair was curling in damp tendrils around his hard-boned face and a single line of sweat arrowed down the front of his T-shirt before disappearing beneath the soft leather of his belt. She put down the bowl of cake mix as she forced her gaze upwards to his face, but that wasn't much better. Why couldn't she just look at those sensual lips without wondering what it would be like to be kissed by them?

'Anything I can do for you, Rafe?'

'You mean, apart from looking as though you'd rather I was anywhere else but here?'

'I told you,' she said stiffly. 'I get uncomfortable if people watch me while I'm working.'

'So you did,' he said softly. 'Well, you won't have to endure my company for much longer because I'm leaving first thing tomorrow.'

'Oh.' Sophie tried to keep her stupid wash of disappointment at bay. 'You are?'

'I am. So I'll be out of your hair once and for all.' He paused. 'I thought you could cook the men a special meal tonight. An early Christmas celebration, if you like. A kind of thank you from me to them for all their hard work over the year. We could open some decent wine—and afterwards go into Corksville for a drink.' His eyes gleamed. 'Think you could manage that, Sophie?'

When he looked at her that way she felt incapable of managing anything except dissolving in a puddle, but somehow Sophie produced an efficient nod of her head. 'Of course!'

She spent the rest of the day rushing around, consulting online recipes as she attempted to make a traditional Christmas dinner for the men, but her thoughts were mostly occupied with what to wear. Because even though she was only there to cook and serve, her cheap dresses and shapeless shorts didn't seem appropriate for a celebration dinner and besides—wasn't there a stupid part of her which *wanted* to dress up? Who wanted Rafe Carter to see her as a real woman for a change, rather than just the fading-into-the-background person she had tried her best to be?

She looked longingly at the one dress which was hanging in her wardrobe and the only outfit she'd brought with her from Isolaverde. It was made to measure by her favourite designer and deceptively simple; she loved the soft blue cotton material, which brought out the colour of her eyes. Just as she loved the fitted bodice and short swinging skirt which brushed her bare thighs as she moved. She slipped it on, along with a pair of strappy sandals, then applied a little mascara and lip gloss. She even left her hair loose for once, clipping it lightly back from her face in case bossy Rafe Carter started giving her a lecture on health and safety regulations while she was cooking.

With barely an hour to spare and the realisation that there were no after-dinner chocolates, she made a last-minute dash into the nearby town of Corksville where Eileen Donahue, the woman who ran the local store, gave her a very curious look.

'I hear the boss man is back,' she said as Sophie put a box of dark chocolate mints on the counter.

Sophie nodded. 'That's right. But he's leaving tomorrow.'

'Shame. The town could do with a little more eye candy.' Eileen gave a sly smile. 'Good-looking man, Rafe Carter.'

Sophie kept her voice neutral. 'So they say.'

'Got himself a permanent woman yet?'

'I really have no idea, Mrs Donahue.'

'Yeah. Heard he plays the field and all.' The storekeeper's eyes narrowed perceptively. 'Still, nice to see you in a dress for a change. Makes you look kind of...*different.*'

It felt like reality slapping her hard across the face and Sophie's fingers stiffened as she pulled a note from her purse.

What did she think she was playing at—risking months of careful anonymity just because she wanted to make some pathetic impression on the boss?

Quickly, she picked up the chocolates and left, but her throat felt dry with anxiety as she drove out of Corksville in a cloud of dust. Had Eileen been looking at her suspiciously as she'd picked up her change, or was she just getting paranoid?

She was putting the finishing touches to the dining-room table when she looked up to find Rafe standing framed in the doorway and she wondered how long he'd been standing there, watching her. He was dressed in a pair of dark trousers and a silk shirt, which was unbuttoned at the neck, all traces of the day's dust and sweat gone. He had the slightly glowing appearance of a man who'd just stepped out of the shower and the sheer intimacy of that fact didn't escape her. And he was looking at her in a way which was making her heart crash painfully against her ribcage.

'Well, well, well.' He blew a soft whistle from between his lips as she placed a folded napkin on one of the placemats. 'It's the Sophie Doukas transformation scene.'

She pretended not to know what he was talking about. 'I'm sorry?'

'The pretty dress. The loose hair. The make-up.'

'You don't like it?'

His lips curved into a smile, which suddenly looked wolfish. Dangerously and attractively so.

'Don't fish for compliments, Sophie. You look very beautiful as I'm sure you're perfectly aware. And the dress is…' he seemed to be having difficulty completing the sentence '…quite something.'

She grabbed another napkin and turned away. 'Thank you.'

Rafe frowned, wondering why her abrupt reaction to a simple compliment was so perplexing—as if she wasn't used to a man telling her she looked beautiful. But then, everything about her was perplexing and he couldn't work out why. He glanced around, taking in the flowers and candles and a starched white tablecloth she must have got from heaven only knew where. Paper chains were looped from one side of the ceiling to the other and, on the plastic Christmas tree, fairy lights gleamed. The overall effect was tacky and yet it was also homely. It was unmistakeably a woman's touch—as if she'd been trying very hard to make the place look comfortable. Something inexplicable twisted at his heart, because Poonbarra was supposed to be about basics. About hard work and getting back to nature. It wasn't supposed to be about *comfort*.

He'd ended up staying longer than planned because he was dreading going back to England for the christening of his half-brother's son. Given his reputation for being the family's habitual no-show—for reasons which were painfully private—nobody could believe he'd agreed to attend in the first place. And in truth, neither could he. He swallowed down the acrid taste which had risen in his throat. He knew that dark and bitter memories were going to be unavoidable, but he told himself he couldn't keep avoiding them for ever. That maybe he needed to ride out the pain once and for all. That maybe you never properly healed unless you faced the reality of what you had done.

But one day had bled into two and then three and delaying his trip had become more...*complex*. He'd underestimated the effect of Poonbarra. Of the peace and calm which always descended on him there—a feeling which had been magnified by the decorative presence of Sophie Doukas...the woman who didn't flirt. The woman who spent her time avoiding him—something which was both novel but ultimately frustrating.

He tried to concentrate on the bottle of wine he was opening, but couldn't seem to stop his gaze from straying to her, no matter how hard he tried. Because she was...a *challenge*? Was that why he couldn't stop thinking about her? Why his hot and erotic dreams had featured plenty of X-rated images of his aloof cook? She must be as aware as he of the sizzling attraction which had sparked between them from the get-go, yet she hadn't acted on it as most women in her position would have done. There had been no unexpected sightings of her around the homestead wearing just a skimpy bath towel. No unexplained 'nightmares' intended to bring him running into her room late at night. She'd done what he'd asked her to do. She'd kept out of his way as much as possible—leaving him frustrating and restless, with a painful ache between his legs.

Yet human nature was a conundrum, that was for sure. When you were used to women flinging themselves at you, it was curiously exciting to discover one who was actively fighting that attraction. In fact, it was the biggest turn-on he knew and it had never happened to him before. He wondered if it was necessary for her to fuss around the bubbling pans quite so much and found himself almost *resenting* Andy and the other workers as they trooped in and sat round the table. All through dinner the overpowering scent of liberally applied aftershave hung cloyingly in the air. Suddenly, the room seemed overcrowded.

Were they in complete thrall to her? Rafe wondered—caught midway between amusement and irritation—as he watched the men lavish praise on her food. Was that why they were acting like tongue-tied adolescents whenever she spoke to them, or appeared with yet another steaming dish held enticingly in front of those magnificent breasts?

He ate and drank very little and when the meal was finished, the men all got up to leave and Andy turned to her.

'You coming to the pub with us, Soph? Let us buy you a beer as a thank you for all your delicious cooking?'

With a smile, she shook her head. 'Not for me, thanks. I'm going to clear up in here and get an early night.'

But Rafe could see her unmistakeable look of...was that *alarm*?...as the men trooped out and he remained seated. He saw the uneasy flicker of her tongue as it edged rather nervously along her bottom lip.

'You're not going to the pub with the others?' she questioned, a touch too brightly.

He shook his head. 'Not me. I've got a long day ahead of me tomorrow.' He gave the ghost of a smile. 'And besides, I might cramp their style.'

'Oh. Right. Well, you'll excuse me if I get on.'

She clattered a pile of plates together and carried them out to the kitchen.

Rafe stretched his arms above his head and knew he ought to move. To go to bed and sleep and figure out how the hell he was going to get through Oliver's christening, especially now that Sharla's presence had been confirmed. The trouble was he didn't want to go anywhere. Not when it was so comfortable sitting here, watching Sophie clear away the dishes. Watching as she busied herself around the table and studiously tried to avoid his gaze. The only trouble was that meant he could stare at her without censure. His eyes lingered on the gleam of her shapely calves and the way the blue cotton dress swished about her bottom as she moved. He found himself thinking longingly about sex and how it might blot out the darkness of his thoughts—and the idea of having sex with Sophie was becoming something of an obsession.

Yet these days he avoided one-night stands—even if he hadn't always made it a rule never to get intimate with employees. Women were tricky enough as lovers without the added complication of them being on the payroll. He'd seen friends and peers get their fingers burned by over-familiarity with staff. Seen how a formerly cool colleague could morph into a bunny-boiling maniac once she'd slipped between the sheets and discovered there wasn't going to be a big rock on her finger as a result. Even if you were honest with a woman from the start and told her you just wanted a no-strings fling, they never believed you. They always thought they'd be the one to change your mind. And how could you escape a rejected lover's wrath if you had to stare at her vengeful face across the other side of the boardroom, or when her manicured fingers were flying across the keyboard?

Or when she was leaning across the table to grab an unused serving spoon and you could smell a trace of her perfume?

Nope. That was an area he had always steered clear of.

So stop looking at her breasts. Stop imagining what it would be like to part those delicious thighs and slip your fingers inside her panties and see how long it would take to make her wet.

'Would you like some coffee, Rafe?'

Her unfathomable accent punctured his thoughts and Rafe met the question in her eyes as he shifted uncomfortably in his seat.

'No,' he said, more curtly than he'd intended. 'I don't want any more to drink. Come and sit down. You've been working all evening. Have you eaten anything?'

'Honestly—I'm fine. I had something before I started serving.'

'Have some chocolate, then. Surely there isn't a woman alive who can resist chocolate?'

'I've still got some clearing up to do.'

'You've done most of it. Leave the rest for now. And that's an order. For heaven's sake, *relax*, Sophie—or is that such an outrageous suggestion?'

Sophie edged towards the chair he was indicating, her heart crashing against her ribcage. *Relax?* He had to be joking. She felt about as relaxed as a mouse which had just glanced up to see a metal trap hovering overhead. Which was slightly ironic for someone who'd spent her whole life being introduced to strangers and putting them at their ease. But for once *she* was the one feeling nervous in the company of a man who was currently pouring her some wine—though she noticed he'd barely touched his own glass all evening.

'Here,' he said, pushing it across the table towards her.

She took the drink and sipped it, grateful for the sudden warmth which flooded through her veins. 'Mmm. This is excellent.'

'Of course it is. Australia produces some of the best wine in the world.' His eyes glittered. 'As well as having the kind of wild beauty which takes the breath away.'

Sophie swirled the wine around and watched it stain the sides of the glass. 'You sound as if you love it. The country, I mean.'

'That's because I do.' He shrugged. 'I always have.'

She looked up from the glass to stare directly

into his eyes. 'Was that why you bought a cattle station here, so far away from England?'

Rafe didn't answer her question straight away because it was a long time since he'd thought about it. What had started out as a bolt-hole from the unbearable had become one of his favourite places. He'd always revelled in the extreme conditions of the Outback and whenever he returned—less and less these days—he settled in right away. He'd come here first for sanctuary, far away from the brutal world he'd left behind. He'd *needed* the hard work and sweat and toil which had helped heal his shattered heart and broken soul. It had been his first stop in a series of places to lay his head without ever really considering any of them home. But then, he'd never had a real home during his childhood, so why should adulthood be any different? His description of himself as a modern-day gypsy had been truthful, though he knew from experience it was an image which turned women on.

Had it turned Sophie on? he wondered. Was that why she was staring at him now, her blue eyes shadowed in the candlelight and those amazing lips slightly parted, as if she wanted him to kiss her? And wasn't the desire to do so almost overwhelming? 'Aren't I supposed to be interviewing *you*,' he said acidly, 'rather than the other way round?'

'Is this an interview, then?' She put her glass down. 'I thought I'd already got the job.'

'Yes, you've got the job. Yet it's interesting,' he mused as he leaned back in his chair, 'that when I asked Andy about your background, he knew nothing about you. And that after several days in your company, I find myself in exactly the same boat. You're a bit of a mystery, Sophie.'

'I thought my role here was to feed the men, not entertain them with my life story?'

'True.' Rafe frowned, thinking that her casual tone was failing to disguise her sudden air of defensiveness. 'Yet apparently, when you arrived, you didn't know one end of a frying pan from the other.'

'I soon learned.'

'Or have a clue how to load the dishwasher.'

She shrugged. 'It's an industrial-sized dish-washer.'

'And you looked at the tin-opener as if it had just landed from outer space.'

'Gosh,' she said sarcastically. 'Just how long did you and Andy spend discussing me?'

'Long enough.'

'And did you come to any conclusions?'

'I did.'

'Which were?'

He stretched out his legs. 'I came to the conclusion that you're someone who's never had to get her hands dirty before,' he observed softly. 'And that maybe you've led a very privileged life up until now.'

Sophie stiffened. How perceptive he was, she thought—her unwilling admiration swept away by a sudden whisper of fear. Because wasn't this what she had dreaded all along—that the cool and clever Englishman would guess she wasn't what she seemed? That he would blow her cover before she was ready to have it blown, and force her into making decisions she still wasn't sure about.

So brazen it out. Challenge him—just as he is challenging you.

She raised her eyebrows. 'But none of the men—or you—have any complaints about my work, do you?'

His eyes glittered. 'Are my questions bothering you, Sophie?'

'Not bothering me so much as boring me, if I may be frank.' She lifted her eyebrows. 'Didn't you tell me when you first arrived that you'd prefer it if I left you alone? That you didn't want me to engage you in conversation just for the sake of it.'

'Did I say that?'

'You know you did,' she said, in a low voice. 'Yet now you're doing exactly that to me!'

'Well, maybe I've changed my mind. Maybe I'm wondering why a young and beautiful woman is hiding herself in the middle of the Outback without making a single phone call or getting any emails.'

She froze. 'What are you talking about?'

'Andy says you don't use a cell-phone. That you haven't received a single letter or card since you've been here—and that you only ever use the Internet very occasionally.'

'I didn't realise I was being constantly monitored,' she said crossly. 'Surely my life is my business.'

'It is, of course. But I'm always intrigued by people who are reluctant to talk about themselves.'

And Sophie suddenly realised why that might be. Because a man like Rafe Carter would have people falling over themselves to tell him everything he wanted to know, wouldn't he? She wondered how he would react if she blurted out the truth. If she told him who she really was. Something told her he wouldn't fawn all over her, the way most people did when they came into close contact with a royal. Something told her he would stay exactly the same—and that was a very tantalising prospect.

Yet she couldn't risk it. No matter how normal he might be in those circumstances, things would inevitably change. He might be angry she hadn't mentioned it before. And what if he inadvertently mentioned it to one of his friends, who mentioned it to someone else—and the wretched press got hold of it? That would be a disaster.

But it was more than his reaction which made Sophie want to keep her secret. She just didn't want to pop this bubble of feeling so *normal*. Of feeling just like anyone else. Why *shouldn't* she talk about herself without mentioning her status? Unless being a princess was the only thing which defined her.

'What exactly do you want to know?' she questioned.

Pushing his wine glass away, Rafe sat back in his chair as he considered her question, but in his heart he knew the answer. He didn't want facts. He wanted her. He'd wanted her from the first moment she'd turned round and looked at him with those big blue eyes. He wanted to crush those amazing lips with his own. To peel that cotton dress from her body and see what delicious treasures lay beneath. To hear her gasping his name as he pushed deep inside her...

He shifted his weight to try to ease his discomfort, realising he was sitting there like some frustrated teenager with a hard-on—and suddenly common sense overrode the primitive needs of his body. What the hell was he thinking of? He forced himself to stand, reminding himself he was leaving tomorrow and that in a week he would scarcely remember her name. 'It's okay, Sophie. You're right. Your life is none of my business.' Suddenly, he smiled. 'But for what it's worth—you're doing a pretty good job.'

It was the praise as much as the smile which got to her and Sophie blinked at him, stupidly moved by his words. She was naturally suspicious of praise because usually it was delivered with some sort of agenda, usually because people were trying to ingratiate themselves with her. But Rafe's words were genuine. He didn't *know* she was a princess. He was saying those things because he meant them. His praise was *real*.

And suddenly she knew she had to get away

from him—before another small act of kindness had her rolling over like a puppy wanting its stomach stroked. Her chair scraped loudly against the wooden floor as she also stood up. 'Thanks,' she said. 'I appreciate it. And in order not to blot my brilliant record, I guess I'd better finish clearing up.'

She went into the kitchen and started washing the glasses, feeling stupidly disappointed when he said goodnight and left her to it. The room felt empty without him. *She* felt empty without him. What had she *wanted* to happen? For him to remove her hands from the soapy water and take her into his arms and start to kiss her?

Yes. That was exactly what she wanted.

Frustrated, she went to her room and took a quick shower before climbing into bed. But despite all her hard work and the thought of the early-morning start, she spent countless minutes lying wide awake in the darkness. Every time she shut her eyes, she was haunted by Rafe's image. By his hard-boned face and powerful body. By the way those steely eyes swept over her, making her stomach turn somersaults. She pushed the cotton sheet from her hot body, going through all the relaxation techniques she knew but nothing seemed to work, until eventually she gave up and got out of bed.

Walking over to the window, she peered out at the beautiful night, where the moon had risen high in the clear and unpolluted sky. She could see its milky glimmer on the surface of the pool and suddenly the thought of a swim seemed irresistible. If she was very quiet she would disturb no one. She could cool herself down and wear herself out and, afterwards, crawl back into bed exhausted.

Pulling on her swimsuit, she slipped her feet into a pair of flip flops and padded quietly outside. Switching on the pool's floodlights, she scanned the surroundings for any of the ubiquitous cane toads who sometimes swam there until the chlorinated water poisoned them, but there were none. Everything was silent except for the ghost-like wailing of a curlew in a distant tree.

Slipping into the water, she swam with strong,

regular strokes which were the result of hours spent practising in the palace pool. She swam until she was pleasantly tired. Floating on her back in the water, she was just thinking about getting out when she heard a splash and, glancing down to the other end of the pool, she froze as she saw a powerful male body swimming beneath the surface of the floodlit water towards her. She held her breath as the man emerged beside her, wet dark hair plastered to his head—his muscular torso painted silver by the moonlight.

'Rafe!' Her heart crashed violently against her ribcage. 'You scared the life out of me!'

'Who did you think it was?'

'A cane toad!' she declared furiously.

'Pretty big cane toad,' he said, a smile curving the edges of his lips.

He dived beneath the water again—swimming several lengths of the pool and back again. It was an impressive display, thought Sophie reluctantly. A deliberate and very macho display and she would have needed to be made of wood not to have responded to it. And Sophie was not made of wood. Far from it. Right then she felt like cream which had been whipped up into soft peaks. Suddenly he emerged beside her again, shaking his head so that little droplets of water showered over her skin.

Tilting his head back, he looked up at the bright canopy of stars. 'Amazing, isn't it?'

Sophie forced herself to follow his gaze. To try to concentrate on the glittering constellations overhead when all she wanted to do was to stare at the magnificence of his wet body. He was so near. So very near. The danger which whispered over her skin was followed by a potent sense of excitement. A sense that she was standing on the edge of the unknown. 'Very beautiful,' she said. The shiver she gave wasn't faked, but it had nothing to do with the temperature and suddenly Sophie felt out of her depth in more ways than one. 'It's…getting cold, isn't it? I'd better go in.'

'Please. Don't let me curtail your swim,' he said softly, his hooded eyes gleaming. 'I'd hate to think I was driving you away. Or that my presence was bothering you.'

Of course it was *bothering* her. He must have known that. Even if his voice hadn't suddenly dipped, the tension which had been growing between them for days now seemed to be reaching a climax. Her breathing had grown so shallow that she barely seemed capable of taking any air into her lungs and Sophie was aware of the blood beating hotly through her veins. He was coming onto her and she wasn't doing a thing to stop him and it was crazy. She knew that.

And yet…

She swallowed.

Why *shouldn't* she respond, when it had been nearly killing her to keep out of his way as much as she had been doing? She'd never done this before. Never had an intimate late-night swim— not even with the Prince to whom she'd been promised in marriage. In fact, she'd never been alone with a man like this—half dressed and totally unguarded—because her life on Isolaverde had been like living in the Dark Ages. She wondered what Rafe Carter would say if he knew she was a stranger to seduction and everything which went with it, but right now she didn't care.

Because for the first time in her life she felt unencumbered by protocol and acutely aware that this opportunity wouldn't come her way again. Her time here was limited and she was hurtling towards an unknown future—a bit like one of the cyclones which would soon dominate and threaten this very region. But none of that seemed to matter now. It was as if everything which had happened in her life up until that moment was about to be tossed aside by a powerful force of nature—in the very alpha shape of her half-naked boss.

With a splash she flipped over, bobbing underneath the water so he couldn't see the pointing of her nipples. But he wasn't looking at her breasts. He was looking at her face and suddenly she was looking right back at his. In the moonlight his eyes gleamed with an intense brilliance which made her stomach flip.

'Rafe?' she said uncertainly, but he silenced her with a shake of his head.

'Come here,' he said, his voice a sudden growl.

She knew he was going to kiss her even before he pulled her against him, against the hard wet planes of his muscular body. She could feel her breasts being crushed against his bare chest and the warmth of his breath just before he crushed her lips beneath his. Her eyelids fluttered to a close as he deepened the kiss and his thumb flicked over the wet stud of her hardening nipple through her swimsuit, making her moan with disbelief that something could feel this good. Because nobody had ever touched her before. Not like this. He slid his hand further down, before letting his fingertips skim over her belly and she wriggled impatiently, wanting him to touch her where she was hot and molten. Made weightless by the water, her thighs parted as if her body was programmed to know exactly how to respond and she sucked in another disbelieving breath as he slipped aside the panel of her swimsuit and pushed his finger deep inside her.

'Rafe,' she gasped against his lips, writhing her hips against him. 'Oh, Rafe.'

Her breathless use of his name seemed to break the erotic spell and when he pulled his hand away she immediately found herself wanting his finger right back where it had been. His eyes were unreadable in the moonlight and his features were harder than she'd ever seen them—his cheekbones two taut slashes against the obvious tension in his face.

'I want to have sex with you,' he said unsteadily. 'And clearly you feel exactly the same way. But there are a few things you need to understand.'

Her heart was thundering so loudly she felt as if she might faint. 'What kind of things?'

'You're staff,' he said bluntly. 'And I don't usually sleep with employees.'

'Oh.' There was a pause as she licked some of the chorine off her lips. 'Well, I guess that's honest, at least.'

'I'm nothing if not honest, Sophie,' he said. 'And if we're going to do this, it has to be on my terms.'

She met his gaze. 'What terms are they?'

'One night. That's all,' he told her, his gaze raking over her. 'No more. No dates. No promises. No happy ever after or follow-up emails. No Christmas present or surprise ticket to New York. And you certainly won't be getting love because I don't do love. I'm out of here tomorrow and it's goodbye. Do you understand what I'm saying?'

Sophie bit her tingling lips as she considered his question. She was caught in the perfect storm of moonlight and desire and opportunity, even though the voice of common sense was urging her to get out while she still could.

But hadn't she always played by the rules and done what was 'right'? And look where it had got her. Deserted by the Prince her people adored and left a laughing stock. She had been placed on a pedestal from the moment of her birth. She was the Princess. People could look but they could never, ever touch. But Rafe had touched. She stared at him. Rafe didn't have a clue who she really was and he didn't care. All she could see was desire in his eyes and a hard, tense body which was calling out to her on the most primitive level of all. He wanted her. Not Princess Sophie. Just Sophie. More than that, she wanted him. Not the billionaire in his shiny helicopter but the elemental man who was making her feel like a real woman for the first time in her life. Him. Rafe Carter.

'I understand,' she said quietly.

His wet brow furrowed into a frown. 'Just like that?'

'Exactly like that.' She shrugged. 'Maybe I want exactly the same thing as you do, Rafe. One night. No strings.'

There was the glint of something predatory in his silvery eyes as he lowered his mouth to kiss her again, only now the kiss was underpinned with a new urgency, which sent the blood beating hotly through her veins. As the water lapped around them he kissed her hard and deep before raising his head, his eyes smoky with lust. 'Then what the hell are we waiting for?' he said roughly, splaying his hand possessively over one wet buttock.

CHAPTER THREE

SOMEHOW RAFE GOT her out of the pool and set her down onto the dripping tiles, his fingertips brushing wet strands of hair away from her face.

'Let's get you inside,' he said, his voice unsteady.

But Sophie hesitated. It seemed so *perfect* right where they were. She was terrified that moving away from that moonlit spot might break the spell—and she couldn't bear that to happen.

'Why do we have to go inside?' she whispered.

He gave a low and silky laugh. 'Call me old-fashioned, but I'd prefer the first time to be in private. Maybe you're one of those women who gets turned on by the prospect of discovery, but if that's the case, don't worry. I can promise you won't need any added extras to make this a night to remember.' He lowered his head to graze his mouth over hers. 'Plus, I didn't exactly arrive carrying condoms. It might have looked a little presumptuous, don't you think?'

His introduction of such an intimate topic silenced her and Sophie let him take her by the hand through a side entrance to an area of the house which she'd never used before and which took them directly into his private quarters. Her damp feet were cooled by the marble floor as she looked around her, blinking in amazement, feeling as if she'd fallen asleep and woken up in another country. It was an incongruous sight—to find such luxury and opulence on an Outback cattle station—and she tried to take it all in as he led her through the different rooms. A study lined with rare, old books led into an enormous sitting room, the walls covered with beautiful paintings of the country he loved so much.

But her admiration of the fixtures and fittings dissolved once he took her into a bathroom as big and as luxurious as any found in her Isolaverdian palace—although with decidedly more masculine overtones. 'It's huge,' she said dazedly.

He paused in the act of sliding a strap of her swimsuit down over one shoulder, his eyes glittering with devilment as they sent a glance slanting in the direction of his groin. 'I assume that wasn't just a flattering innuendo?'

She prayed he couldn't see the faint rise of colour in her cheeks. She prayed he wouldn't discover that she was new to all this. 'I'm talking about your suite of rooms,' she said primly.

His fingers moved towards the second strap. 'You mean you didn't come peeping, before I arrived?'

'No, I…*oh…*' She bit her lip as he tugged the damp fabric down over her breasts. 'I certainly did not.'

He bent to fasten his lips over one cold nipple and then the other, tantalising the acutely sensitised and puckering skin with the faint graze of his teeth. She looked down to see his dark hair contrasted against her pale skin and spangles of pleasure rippled over her body as she buried her fingers in the damp tendrils.

A sudden fervour seemed to grip him as he finished peeling off her swimsuit before removing his own wet shorts and towelling her dry. And before she really had time to register that they were both naked, he picked her up and carried her into a vast bedroom, putting her down on a king-size bed. Part of her felt like a sacrificial lamb as she lay there, outlined against his sheets in the silvery moonlight—but the heated hunger of her body was powerful enough to make any anxieties melt away. Plus, he was just so beautiful. Powerful and strong, with long, muscular legs and narrow hips, his buttocks a paler colour than the deeper olive glow of his skin.

Sophie licked her lips. She'd never seen a naked man before—not unless you counted the famous statues which brought visitors flocking to the Isolaverdian national museum during the winter months. And those naked men were made of marble, usually with a fig leaf covering their modesty. It occurred to her that Rafe would have needed an entire bunch of fig leaves to cover *his* most intimate part and that maybe she should have been daunted by the stiff, proud column of his erection. But she wasn't. As he moved over her, she just felt...*eager.*

'Well, just look at you,' he said unsteadily, as his fingertip trailed a slow path from her neck to her belly button. 'Aren't you gorgeous?'

She gave a wriggle of pleasure. 'Am I?'

'You know damned well you are. A million men must have told you so.'

His remark brought reality creeping into the room but Sophie didn't want reality. She wanted to *feel*, not to think. She wanted to feel a man's fingers on her skin. To be intimate with a man who desired her, not because of her position or her status—but because they had a powerful chemistry which could not be denied.

So she coiled her arms around his neck and looked up at him, invitation vying with reprimand in her voice.

'I don't want to talk about other men right now,' she said honestly.

His smile was hard as he cupped one breast with possessive arrogance, grinding his hips a little, so that she could feel the hard brush of his erection against her skin.

'Me neither,' he said.

He began to stroke her, the slow graze of his fingers exploring her. She gasped when his thumb first brushed against the tight bud above so much honeyed warmth, but within seconds she was hungrily anticipating more. Each practised stroke of his finger took her deeper—deep into a place of almost unimaginable pleasure and she heard him laugh as she gasped his name out loud. It felt as if her body was opening up to him, sensation flooding through her with relentless, rhythmical beats, and Sophie began to move restlessly, wanting more. And although he must have sensed her impatience, he took his time—eking out the pleasure, second by delicious second. He stroked her until she was writhing beneath him and, although she was eager to explore his body, she was shy about touching him *there*. Because what if she did the wrong thing? What if she destroyed the magic with some clumsy caress? Her lips sought his as she lifted her hips up, so that she could feel the weight of his erection pressing into her belly.

He made some little curse beneath his breath as he drew away and reached inside the drawer of the nightstand and Sophie stiffened as he tore open a little foil packet, scarcely able to believe that it was going to happen. After all the years of waiting, of saving her innocence for a man whose parents had bartered with her parents for her hand in marriage, she was about to lose her virginity in the anonymity of the Australian Outback, with the man who was paying her wages. A man who had promised her no tomorrows and scorned the idea of love. And yet she didn't care. It was as if she'd been living in a dark cave which was about to be flooded by something brilliant and beautiful—and her life would never be the same again.

She watched as he began to stroke on the rubber and lifted his gaze, curving her a complicit smile as if silently acknowledging her enjoyment of the floorshow. Would he be shocked if he knew what she was *really* thinking—that she'd never seen either a condom or an erection before? Was he going to be disappointed once the truth was out and wouldn't it be better to tell him now?

Instinct overrode her brief spike of conscience as she coiled her arms around his neck. Because this was an education, she reminded herself fiercely. A rite of passage. Something she needed to do to shake off the shackles of innocence and join the ranks of real women. Nothing more than that. This was what modern, normal people did. They met, they were attracted to one another—and they had sex. Why spoil it by revealing all her hang-ups and compromise her anonymity in the process?

He was moving over her and it felt slightly scary as he guided himself towards her—to where she was so hot and sticky. She tried not to tense up as he eased himself inside her, but he was so big she couldn't help herself gasping out. For a moment he stilled, lifting his head to look at her—an expression of incomprehension etched onto his dark features.

His one-word question was incredulous. 'You—?'

'Yes,' she gasped as her hips jerked forwards all of their own accord, so that he went in even deeper. 'But don't stop, Rafe. Please don't stop.'

Rafe gave a strangled groan as he went deeper into her tight heat. How could he possibly have stopped when she was raining urgent kisses all over his shoulder and squeezing her pelvic muscles in a way which instantly made him want to come?

This really *was* just going to be once, he told himself grimly—so he had better make it something she would remember for the rest of her life. The best sex she would ever have. The only sex she would ever have—with him. Holding back his own hunger, he began to tease her clitoris with his finger as he thrust in and out of her, making her moan with pleasure—her cries getting louder with each penetration. He halted and lifted his head to look at her as a cold kind of anger rippled over his skin.

'Keep quiet,' he ordered. 'I don't want you waking the men.'

But she didn't—or couldn't—keep quiet. Least of all when she began to come and he sensed that her gasps of disbelief were going to morph into cries of ecstasy. So he bent his head to kiss her, and the frantic touch of her lips seemed to intensify his own orgasm—and suddenly it was *his* cry being stifled by *her* kiss and the balance of power had shifted and he didn't like that either.

He could feel her contracting around him as his body jerked like a puppet whose strings had been cut, and only when nature had finished with him and emptied him of all his seed did he have the strength to pull out. To roll away from her and close his mind to the rapturous look on her face as her eyelids fluttered to a close. To ignore the ruffled hair and dreamy expression of someone who had just experienced sex for the first time. Because although he wanted to lick her breasts and slide his hand between her thighs again and make her come all over his fingers, he didn't intend touching her until she'd given him some kind of explanation.

A virgin! Dazedly, he shook his head. Whoever would have guessed it, when she'd agreed to have casual sex without any degree of hesitation? She'd been so up for it that they could have done it in the swimming pool. Or in the garden. If he'd laid her out on the kitchen table where she buttered bread each morning, he reckoned she still would have given him the green light. Why, she'd acted like someone completely at ease with her own sexuality—right up to the moment when he'd thrust inside her and she'd made that broken little cry. Why the hell hadn't she told him she was innocent—and at least given him the option of whether or not he wanted to be the first?

And yet it had been amazing, hadn't it? The most amazing sex he could remember?

Pushing away the rogue thought, he didn't speak until he was certain his words would come out as measured and controlled. But even then his throat felt constricted and he could feel another rush of heat to his groin as he remembered easing into her slick tightness.

'You're certainly a woman of surprises,' he said. 'You don't happen to have any more hidden up your sleeve?'

Sophie froze as she realised it was probably the most astute question he could have asked in the circumstances. *What would he say if he realised what else she wasn't telling him*? She kept her eyes shut, not daring to open them, afraid of what they might reveal—when she wasn't even sure herself. She felt…what?

She swallowed.

Complete? Yes. Satisfied? Very. She felt shy yet strangely confident, because she'd done it and it had *worked*. She'd had sex! She'd had an orgasm! Underneath all the glitz and the unusual upbringing, she was no different from any other woman—and that thought gave her hope for the future. It made her feel strong. As if she was capable of pretty much anything she set her mind to. And Rafe had touched her as she'd always dreamed a man might do. Not in a reverential way. Not treating her as if she were made of porcelain or making her acutely aware of her 'blue blood'—but treating her just like a woman. And before he'd made love to her, he'd hugged her, hadn't he? Held her close. He'd picked her up and carried her. Cradled her tight against his wet chest—and that had blown her away nearly as much as the sex, because she wasn't used to physical contact. Even as a child, her parents had never been demonstrative. The Queen used to appear before dinner—all dressed up in her finery—and one of the palace nannies would troop the royal children in for a quick kiss goodnight. Why, she'd been touched more tonight than in her entire life.

Sophie sighed as she wriggled against the rumpled bedsheet, not sure whether she wanted to slide beneath it with her happy, private thoughts, or to dance around the room in celebration. But what she wanted most of all was to tiptoe her fingers over Rafe's silky flesh and have him kiss her again. She wanted him to wipe that curiously judgemental expression from his face—

because what did it matter that she'd never had sex before? She wondered what the etiquette for dealing with a situation like this was and how ironic that she, an expert in etiquette, should be at such a loss.

Well, she wasn't going to cower away like someone who was ashamed, because she wasn't. Maybe she should just let him know how *much* she'd enjoyed it and then maybe he would do it to her all over again.

She felt liquid heat pooling low in her stomach as her eyelashes fluttered open and she was unprepared for the punch of emotion she felt as she looked at him—the man who up until a few minutes ago had been deep inside her. He looked the same, and yet he seemed different—but then she'd never seen him naked in the moonlight before, or softened by the intimacy of sex. Her gaze drifted over his powerful dark body, outlined against the rumpled white sheets, because surely what had just happened gave her the right to study him like this. Something melted deep inside her as she felt her heart skip a beat. How

was it possible to want him again so quickly—
and did he want her, too?

Her tongue slid out to moisten her lips. 'That
was—'

'Don't tell me.' His voice was a hard and cyni-
cal drawl. 'Amazing? Wonderful? Women usually say it was the best sex they've ever had,
although I suppose in your case that would be
difficult to gauge since it's the *only* sex you've
ever had.'

Sophie went very still, thinking he must be
making a joke—and a joke in very poor taste—
to discuss his other lovers at such a sensitive
time. But as her eyes sought his face she could
see no trace of humour there and she realised
that he seemed *irritated*. Disenchantment whispered over her but she didn't show it—grateful
for years of social training, which meant she was
able to return his gaze with a cool impartiality.
'You sound disappointed, Rafe. Do you have a
problem with the fact that I was a virgin?'

'Only the same kind of problem I might have if

I took a ride in a car with somebody who hadn't bothered to tell me they were a learner driver.'

His cutting words shattered the last few traces of bliss and Sophie stared straight ahead at the unfamiliar wall of the moonlit bedroom. 'Thanks for the comparison,' she said flatly.

'Why the hell have you never had sex before?' he demanded. He shook his head in disbelief. 'You're young. You're beautiful. You were clearly up for it. And this is the twenty-first century.'

Sophie swallowed. Now was the time to come clean. To say what she would need to repeat at least once, because he would think she was making it up.

You might have been living in the twenty-first century, but I certainly wasn't. Because I was born a royal and betrothed to one of the world's most eligible men and part of the deal was that I would go to him as a virgin on my wedding night.

And then what?

A nightmare, that was what. Once she'd convinced him she wasn't a complete fantasist, she would be obliged to dredge up a past she was trying to move on from. She would be forced into a truth she didn't want to have to face— that she was a princess with an unknown future. And even worse—what if he suddenly became very interested? True, he didn't seem the type—but you never *really* knew. Lots of people were turned on by palaces and crowns and a status which couldn't be bought, or earned. And wouldn't it only reinforce her plummeting self-esteem if he decided he wanted her for *what* she was, rather than *who* she was?

Suddenly she was filled with an overwhelming desire to temper his arrogance. To see if she could unsettle *him* for a change. 'Maybe I was just waiting to meet the right man,' she said innocently, watching as he sat up in bed, quickly covering the lower part of his body with the rumpled bedsheet. But not before she'd noticed that he was aroused again and for some reason that gave her a fleeting feeling of triumph.

'I think we'd better get one thing clear, Sophie,' he said as a pulse worked frantically at his temple. 'The sex we just had was amazing. More than amazing—especially as it was your first time. You don't have enough experience to know that, but let me assure you it's true.' He paused, as if picking his words carefully. 'But the fact remains that I'm not in the market for any kind of commitment. I meant every word of what I said to you in the pool. This changes nothing.'

She widened her eyes. 'Oh?'

'I don't want you having any unrealistic expectations, that's all. I'm not the kind of man who is blown away by the fact you were a virgin—I don't have some primitive, chest-thumping desire to shout it from the rooftops. It doesn't mean anything to me and neither do you. Sorry to be so blunt, but it saves any kind of misunderstanding. I'm not looking for a partner and even if I was, that partner wouldn't be you. I told you that I believe in honesty and I'm being honest now. We have very different lives,' he added, almost gently. 'You're a cook on some kind of late-on-set gap year and I'm a globetrotting CEO. Think about it.' He gave a shrugging kind of smile. 'It could never work.'

Oh, the arrogant, *arrogant* man! Sophie resisted the urge to pick up the nearest hard object and hurl it at him, before telling herself that behaving rashly wouldn't improve anything and it would compromise any remaining dignity. But at least his attitude made her decision easier. There would be no confidences shared with this particular Englishman. She wasn't going to tell him a single thing about herself—why should she, when he obviously couldn't wait to get away from her?

Some of her inbuilt royal confidence came rushing back as she returned his stare. 'I think you flatter yourself,' she said coolly as she got out of bed and picked up the discarded towel which was lying in a heap on the floor. 'I agree with every word you say. It was nothing but an initiation to sex and a pretty amazing one. So thanks for that—but rest assured that I'm not looking for commitment either. I told you that in the pool. Maybe I should have let on that I was a virgin but I didn't want to destroy the mood. And since you're such a busy globetrotting CEO who is flying out of here tomorrow, I'd better let you get some peace so you can sleep. Goodnight, Rafe.' She flashed him a smile. 'Sweet dreams.'

And Sophie felt a very different kind of satisfaction as she saw the expression of disbelief on Rafe Carter's face just before she turned and walked out of his bedroom.

CHAPTER FOUR

RAFE WAS WOKEN by the insistent sound of his phone vibrating and he stifled a groan as he picked it up. It was one of several he owned but the only one whose number was given to those closest to him. He glanced at the flashing screen to see that it was William, one of his assistants, calling from New York. He frowned. William was in a completely different time zone and had strict instructions not to disturb him unless absolutely necessary.

He hit the button and waited.

'Rafe?'

'Of course it's me! Who else did you think it would be? It's five o'clock in the flaming morning!' Rafe answered, his mood not enhanced by the sight of Sophie's discarded swimsuit lying on the floor of the en-suite bathroom. Or by the fact that an image of her face had been haunting him for hours, meaning that he'd only fallen into a fitful sleep a restless hour ago.

A rush of heat flooded through his groin as he remembered the sex of the night before. Remembered her beautiful body laid out like a feast on top of his sheets with those big blue eyes looking up at him and her long legs parted in invitation. And she had been a *virgin*, he reminded himself grimly. She hadn't bothered telling him *that* before she had thrust her wet breasts against him in the swimming pool, had she?

Because women had their secrets, he thought bitterly. Every damned one of them keeping stuff hidden away and not caring about the consequences.

And sometimes their secrets became your secrets and they gnawed away deep inside you until there was nothing but a dark and empty hole.

He sat up, his fingers tightening around the phone. 'I thought I told you I wasn't to be disturbed unless absolutely necessary,' he bit out.

His assistant's voice grew serious. 'This is very necessary, Rafe.'

Rafe stilled, because even though he came from the world's most dysfunctional family, they were still family. Yet if somebody was ill, it wouldn't be his assistant ringing him. It would be Amber, or one of his half-brothers, surely. 'What's the matter?' he demanded. 'Is someone sick?'

'No. Nobody's sick.'

'What, then?' questioned Rafe impatiently.

There was a split-second pause. 'That girl you've got working at the station.'

'Sophie,' said Rafe instantly and then could have cursed himself. Surely he should have taken longer than a nanosecond to recall the name of one of his itinerant workers. 'The cook.'

'She's not a cook.'

'She may have only the most basic of culinary skills, but I can assure you she most certainly is.'

'She's a princess.'

There was a pause. 'William, have you been drinking?'

'She's a princess from Isolaverde,' his assistant continued doggedly. 'One of the world's richest islands. Gold, diamonds, petroleum, natural gas, uranium. They hold some international yacht race every year. They've even—'

'I get the idea, William. And I've heard of it. Get on with it.'

'She's young and beautiful—'

You're telling me. 'The *facts*,' bit out Rafe.

'She was engaged to some prince. Prince Luciano of Mardovia—known as Luc. Bit of a player—lived on another Mediterranean island—known each other since they were kids. Just before the engagement was due to be announced he goes and makes some English dressmaker pregnant. Big scandal. He was forced to marry the dressmaker—so the wedding with Princess Sophie had to be called off. And that's when she disappeared.'

'Disappeared?' repeated Rafe slowly, his mind spinning as he tried to get his head round the relevant facts. Not just the fact that the name Luc rang a distant bell in his memory, but a far more worrying one. He'd just had sex with a virgin *princess*?

'Into thin air. She ran away. Or rather, flew away. Nobody really knew about it because her brother instigated an information lockdown. And no one had any idea where she was. At least, not until now.' Another pause. 'They know she's at Poonbarra, Rafe.'

'And how...?' Rafe drew in a deep breath. 'How the hell do they know that?'

'Seems like Eileen Donahue—that's the woman who runs the general store in Corksville—recognised Sophie yesterday. Said she was, and I quote, "All dolled up for a change" and that she seemed "familiar". So she looked her up on the Internet—and what do you know? Sophie *is* familiar. She's royal, no less. Eileen contacted one of the papers in Brisbane and I'm afraid the rest is exactly how you imagine it would be. The journalists did their research and I'm ringing to say that you can expect a deputation of the world's press on your doorstep before too long.'

Rafe's fingers clasped the phone so tightly that he heard his knuckles crack. 'That can't be allowed to happen, William,' he said in a low voice. 'I don't want a circus invading town. Poonbarra is a place of privacy. The one place in the world where I am guaranteed peace. I want you to kill this story and I want you to kill it now.'

'I don't see how that's going to be possible, boss. It's already got legs.'

'Well, just get me out of here before they arrive.' Rafe's voice was cold.

There was a pause. 'Let me see what I can do.'

Rafe swore as he cut the connection and resisted the desire to crush the phone in the palm of his hand. Pushing back the sheet, he got out of bed, trying to temper his mood and think rationally—even though all he wanted to do was storm through the homestead to find Sophie Doukas and give her a piece of his mind. Another wave of anger enveloped him. Not only had she kept her innocence secret, but she'd omitted to tell him that she was a royal. *A royal on the run!* Deceitful woman. *Scheming* woman.

Anger and resentment washed over him but he could still smell her on his skin and taste her in his mouth and it was tantalising and distracting. Even the thought of her was making his body grow hard, so he forced himself to stand beneath the icy jets of the shower, which did little to cool his heated blood. Dragging a razor across his jaw, he somehow managed to nick his skin in the process and that only increased his frustration.

Pulling on a shirt and a pair of trousers, he went looking for her but, since it wasn't quite six, the house was completely silent and there were no sounds of clatter coming from the kitchen. His rage mounting, he strode along the quiet corridors—forcing himself to knock on her door even though part of him just wanted to kick it open in a primitive way, which was not his usual style at all.

She was already up and dressed and answered the knock immediately but her eyes were hooded and cautious when she saw it was him. She was wearing a pair of shapeless cotton trousers and a T-shirt, yet all he could think about was the magnificence of her naked body and the way she'd cried out when he'd opened her legs and entered her. And once again he was furious with himself for the hot surge of lust which flooded through his bloodstream, knowing that he should be concentrating on her lies and subterfuge, not her undeniable physical appeal.

'Rafe,' she said, her fingers flying to the base of her throat where he could see a small pulse hammering.

'Oh, don't worry,' he said, with a disdainful curl of his lips. 'I haven't come here for sex.'

'Oh? Then why have you come here?'

She tilted her chin in a defiant gesture and suddenly Rafe wondered how he could have been so dense. *Of course she was someone*—hadn't that been apparent from the start? A diamond in the rough—that had been his initial reaction on seeing her and he had been right. And when he stopped to think about it, her high-born status had been apparent in every gesture she made.

It had been there in the way she moved and the way she walked. In her flawless skin and heart-shaped face and the thick, lustrous bounce of her hair. She was a princess. Of course she was. A runaway virgin princess who had chosen him as her first lover.

Why?

'I'm still trying to get my head around what happened last night,' he said. 'About the fact that you let a virtual stranger take your virginity. And wondering if there's anything else you've omitted to tell me?'

Sophie went very still, because something in his eyes told her the game was up—but still she clung to her fake freedom for a few last, precious seconds. She tried to convince herself it was her own guilty conscience making her think he'd found out who she really was—but that was impossible. Just because he'd been deep inside her body the night before, didn't mean he'd suddenly developed the ability to read her mind, did it? How could he *possibly* know?

'Like what?' she questioned nonchalantly.

Her words seemed to make something inside him snap and he took a step towards her. 'Oh, sweetheart,' he said softly. 'Why do women find it impossible to give a straight answer? Why is deceit always their default setting? I gave you the chance to tell me the truth, but surprise surprise—you chose not to take it. I'm talking about the fact that you're a princess—and that the world's press know you're here.'

'No,' she whispered, her fingers moving from her neck to her lips.

'Yes,' he said grimly.

She shook her head. 'They can't know. I've been here for months and been left in peace. How...how did they find out?'

'Apparently, the woman who runs the store at Corksville recognised you.'

And Sophie could have wept. How could she have been so *stupid*? Why hadn't she just behaved the same way she'd always behaved with her nondescript clothes and her hair hidden beneath a big hat? But, no. Rafe Carter had returned and the lure of feminine pride had been too strong to resist. For once she'd worn a dress. For once she'd applied mascara and left her hair loose. Vanity and desire had been her downfall. She had discarded her habitual disguise and someone had identified her. She had nobody to blame but herself.

But her regret was fleeting. There was no time for regrets. No time for anything except to work out what she did next.

'I'm sorry,' she said.

'It's a bit late for that,' he snapped.

'What else do you expect me to say?' she said, and walked back inside her bedroom. 'Excuse me. I have a lot to do.'

But Rafe had followed her and was reaching out to catch hold of her wrist, and even in the middle of all her confusion and fear—*even in the middle of all that*—she could still feel her hotly instinctive response to his touch. She wanted him to pull her close. To kiss her again. To put his tongue inside her mouth and his erection deep inside her body and make her feel all those things he'd made her feel last night.

'What I can't work out is how you got here,' he bit out. 'A royal princess travelling all the way from Isolaverde to the east coast of Australia without anyone knowing.'

Sophie snatched her hand away and stared at the faint imprint his fingers had left on her wrist. Her journey here seemed like a dream now. Like something out of an adventure film. But why *not* tell him? Surely it would reinforce the fact that she had been brave and resilient—and she could be those things all over again *if only she believed in herself.*

'The man I was meant to marry made another woman pregnant.'

'So my assistant just informed me.'

Sophie's mouth pleated in dismay as she experienced that old familiar feeling of people talking about her behind her back. 'It was the biggest outrage to happen in years and everyone seemed to have an opinion about it,' she continued. 'It was *claustrophobic* on the island and I knew I had to get away. No bodyguards or ladies-in-waiting, or people fussing round me.

I just wanted to be on my own for the first time in my life, to lick my wounds and decide what I wanted to do next. But more than that, I wanted to feel like a normal person for once. To shake off all the royal trappings and do something on my own.'

'I'm not interested in the pop psychology behind your actions,' he said coldly. 'More the practicalities.'

'My brother was away on a hunting trip,' she said slowly. 'So I left him a note saying I was leaving and not to try to find me. And then I persuaded one of the palace pilots to fly me to the west coast of the USA.'

He frowned. 'How the hell did you persuade him to do that?'

She shrugged. 'It shouldn't take too much of a stretch of your imagination to work it out. I made it worth his while.'

'Of course you did. And you would have needed to pay him a lot of money,' he said cynically. 'Since presumably smuggling you out of there meant the end of his flying career at the palace?'

'I didn't force him to agree!' She felt a sudden flicker of rebellion. 'He was happy to do it.'

'So what happened next?' he said, in a hard voice.

'He took me to one of the smaller Californian ports and introduced me to a friend of his—a man named Travis Matthews—who had a boat big enough to cross the Pacific. And that's what I did.'

Now he was staring at her in disbelief. 'You *crossed the Pacific*?'

'I'm a good sailor,' she said defensively. 'I love boats more than anything. And there was a crew of six, so I was just an extra. It took us weeks. It was…'

As her voice faltered he frowned. 'It was what?'

Sophie swallowed. This had been the bit she hadn't counted on. The bit which had soothed her wounded ego and hurt pride and put it all in perspective. The sheer beauty of being that far out at sea—the ever-changing ocean and the bright stars at night. And a sense of freedom she'd never known before. It had been a heady experience and one she would never forget.

She looked at the sculpted lines of Rafe's hard face, at the steely grey eyes, which last night had darkened with hunger, yet today were glittering with fury. Why tell him things which would bore him rigid? Stick to the facts, she told herself fiercely. The *practicalities*.

'It was an interesting experience,' she said.

'And when you got to Australia? What then?'

She shrugged. 'We docked at Cairns where Travis had a contact of his pick me up and drive me out this way. En route I stopped off at a store and bought an entire new wardrobe.'

'Discount clothes?' he questioned dryly, with a sardonic glance at her outfit.

'Exactly that. Nothing which could possibly identify me.' Reflectively she rubbed the hem of her cheap T-shirt between thumb and forefinger. 'And you know what? That was a liberation, too. Putting on something which was indistinguishable from what the woman at the checkout was wearing made me feel that I was the same as everyone else for the first time in my life.'

Rafe shook his head. 'Except that most women at the checkout don't have a multimillion-dollar trust fund bolstering up their little *adventures*,' he said sarcastically, before something occurred to him. Something which chimed with the nagging memory in his mind. 'Did you *know* this was my cattle station?'

She hesitated and he saw an uncomfortable look cross her face. 'Why do you ask?'

'No more lies or evasion, Sophie,' he bit out. 'Just tell me the truth.'

'Yes, I'd heard about your station.'

'How?'

She shrugged. 'The man I was supposed to marry is called Prince Luc and your sister Amber's husband is an art dealer who once sold him a painting. Luc was telling me about Conall Devlin marrying into the Carter family—about how you're all scattered across the world and how none of you conform. He mentioned that you were some bigshot entrepreneur who had a huge cattle station.'

'And you liked the sound of me, did you?' he questioned arrogantly.

'Hardly,' came her frosty retort. 'The thing that attracted me was the fact that you were never here. I knew from talking to Travis that most cattle stations employed a cook and that I could probably teach myself.'

'But we already had a cook working here,' he said.

She flushed a little. 'I know you did. But I met her for a drink and…'

'Let me guess. You offered her money to go earlier than planned?'

Flushing a little, she nodded. 'That's right.'

'Oh, Sophie. How easy it is for you to delude yourself,' he said softly. 'For all your commendable announcements about wanting to be the same as everyone else, it must give you a pretty big buzz to realise you can buy pretty much anything you want if you throw enough money at it.'

'Are you telling me you've never used your own fortune to do exactly the same?'

Rafe stiffened as he met the challenge in her eyes and an unwanted feeling of regret coursed through him. How would she react if he told her that the only things he'd ever wanted were things which money could never buy? Things which could never have a price attached to them. Things he had lost and could never get back. He shook his head. 'This is your story, not mine,' he said bitterly. 'Get on with it.'

'I've told you everything you need to know.' She walked over to the top of the wardrobe to pull down a huge rucksack, which she threw on top of the bed. 'Just console yourself with the fact that you won't have to put up with me for much longer!'

'What do you think you're doing?'

'What does it look like I'm doing? I'm leaving. I can't stay here,' she said, tugging open a drawer and pulling out a stack of T-shirts, which she began to layer haphazardly in the rucksack. 'If I stay it'll be too much hassle for you.'

'Oh, please. Spare me the spin. I don't imagine you're leaving out of the goodness of your heart, are you, little Miss *Princess*?'

Sophie heard the venom in his voice and thought about the way he'd touched her last night. The way he'd made her feel so safe and *protected*. As if she was capable of anything. She remembered the way she'd trembled with delight as he'd explored her skin with his fingers and his mouth. The way she'd gasped with pleasure with each deep stroke he'd made. She had taken a long time to have sex for reasons which were complex and unique, but Rafe Carter had been the perfect lover—even if now he was looking at her as if she were something he'd found squashed beneath the sole of his shoe.

And surely what happened last night had been about more than sexual liberation. She had given herself to him freely—so didn't that give her the right to treat him as an equal and be treated as an equal herself?

'Is it fair to criticise me because I was born

with a title?' she said. 'Something which is completely outside my control.'

'Would you prefer that I criticised you for your
deceit instead? For failing to tell me who you
really were?'

'But I couldn't tell you,' she said simply. 'How
could I? I couldn't tell anyone—it would have
made it impossible for me to stay here. Surely
you can see that. It would have altered everything.'

'And of course, if you'd told me, particularly
the part about your lack of sexual experience...'
his eyes glinted '...then at least I would have
had a choice about whether I wanted to be used
as an experimental lover in your big round-the-
world adventure.'

'It wasn't like that!' she said fiercely.

'No? You chose me because we'd forged a deep
bond in less than a week of knowing one another?'

'I actually wasn't analysing it very much at
all—I was just going with the flow. And aren't
you forgetting that there were two people in-

volved in what happened?' she questioned quietly. 'Or just preferring to forget your part in it?'

'So what was it? Did I tick all the right boxes, Sophie?' He began to tap each one of his fingers in turn. 'Rich, single, hot and therefore the perfect candidate to give the rejected royal her first taste of sexual pleasure?'

Flinging a belt on top of the T-shirts, Sophie lifted her head, grabbing at the streak of anger which flashed through her because surely anger was better than buckling under these sudden feelings of vulnerability and sadness which were bubbling up inside her. 'You bastard,' she whispered shakily, but Rafe Carter didn't look in the least bit shocked by her first ever public use of a swear word. The only emotion she could see flickering in his hard grey eyes was bitter cynicism.

'Yeah. For a while I was exactly that. A bastard,' he drawled. 'My father didn't marry my mother until three days after I was born. As it turned out, they should never have bothered.'

His phone started to vibrate in his pocket and

he slid it out to take the call, listening in silence as Sophie continued to pack the rucksack.

'Where are you planning to go?' he questioned, once the connection had been cut.

She didn't look up, terrified now that her vulnerability would be impossible to hide. 'I haven't really thought about it.'

'Well, start thinking!' He felt a flicker of temper. 'You're not protected by your royal status now, Sophie. You're out in the middle of Queensland with a limited choice of transport available, no matter how much money you're suddenly able to produce. That was my assistant on the phone. He says your presence in my Outback home is generating a lot of interest on a quiet news day—not least because I'm just about to mount a bid for one of Malaysia's biggest cell-phone networks and there's been a lot of opposition to the deal.' His mouth twisted. 'So thanks very much for that.'

'I'm sorry this has impacted on you because it was never intended to,' she said. 'But I'll be out of your life soon, Rafe. You can put all this down to experience and forget it ever happened. Which is precisely what you wanted in the first place, isn't it?'

She zipped up the rucksack and swept her tumbled hair away from flushed cheeks and Rafe was reminded of the way she'd moved over him the night before. He remembered the brush of her pubic hair as he'd tangled his fingers in it. The beat of her heart and how tight she'd felt. The way he'd kissed away her cries of pleasure. And damn it if he couldn't feel the sudden debilitating jerk of sexual desire as he visualised pushing her down on that bed and ripping open the ugly cotton trousers and doing it to her all over again.

'If only it was that easy,' he growled. 'What do you think it's going to do for my reputation if I leave you here to fend for yourself among the rabble of newshounds who are due to arrive?'

'Heaven forbid I might damage your reputation!'

'You might not care about my reputation,

sweetheart, but I do. And I'm not letting you go anywhere on your own.'

She tilted her chin in defiance. 'That sounds awfully like an order to me.'

'At least that's something you've got right. Because if that's what it takes to make you see sense, then it's an order.' His eyes bored into her. 'What's the matter, Little Princess? Not used to somebody else telling you what to do?'

She stared at the door behind him, as if planning to make a rush for it. 'If you must know, I've spent my whole life being told what I can and can't do and this is the first time I've ever been able to decide things on *my* terms. So please don't trouble yourself with concerns about my personal safety, Rafe. I can have some Isolaverdian bodyguards sent out here to look after me.'

'And how long is that going to take?' he demanded. 'Even if your rarefied palace protection people knew how to cope with life in the bush, which I doubt. The situation could dissolve into complete farce with people suffering from heatstroke or getting spooked by some animal they've never seen before, or worse. Is that what you want?'

Sophie bit her lip. She didn't know *what* she wanted. Well, in a stupid way she did. She wanted to rewind time so that she was back in his arms. She wanted to feel like a normal woman again. And that was never going to happen.

'I don't know,' she admitted, hating the sudden break in her voice.

Rafe stiffened as he steeled himself against that unexpected trace of vulnerability. Because it was all an act, he reminded himself grimly. Everything about her was false. And until her playboy fiancé had jumped ship, she'd presumably been given everything she wanted, no matter how much she might protest otherwise. Well, she was about to learn that around here he was the one who called the shots.

'You're going to have to come with me,' he said, an idea slowly forming in his head. 'And perhaps we can each do one another a favour at the same time.'

'Come where?' She narrowed her eyes suspiciously. 'And what kind of a favour?'

Rafe stared down at the bulging rucksack as it occurred to him that this—like all bad situations—could be turned into an advantage. Couldn't the unbearable prospect of having to face Sharla again be diluted by taking Sophie to his nephew's christening? Because the presence of a beautiful princess would easily trump the fact that one of the world's most famous supermodels was going to be there.

Haunting him with what she'd done. Or, rather, what she had failed to do.

'To England,' he said. 'I have a family christening I can't get out of. This is the first time the Carters have been together in a long time and I'm not looking forward to it.'

'Why not?'

'Why is none of your business,' he snapped. 'Let's just say that family reunions have never been my thing. But since there's safety in numbers, you can be my plus one. You get safe passage out of here, and I get someone who can deflect some of the attention away from me.'

'But I don't want to go to England for a family christening—and I certainly don't want to be your "plus one".'

'No? Then what else are you going to do?'

Sophie fished around for a suitable answer but with a sinking heart realised her options were limited. They always were. She didn't want to go home—not right now, when the people of her country would still look at her with sympathy in their eyes. Yet anywhere else would only emphasise her lone status—especially around Christmas time. Wouldn't travelling with Rafe stop the press from getting too close, while she decided what she was going to do next? Hadn't she proved that she could cope with hard work and be resourceful? She was young and fit and there was a great big world out there. Why shouldn't she use this opportunity to decide how best to embrace her new life?

She met the steely gleam of his eyes, thinking about the harsh things he'd said to her. She didn't like him very much but something told her she'd be safe with him. Not because they shared a special connection because of what had happened last night, but because he was strong and powerful. A man like this could protect you, she thought wistfully. And he could make you want him, even if you knew that wanting him was the last thing you needed.

She could do nothing to stop the ripple of sexual awareness which had started spreading over her body but she did her best not to think about it. His offer made perfect sense but she could only accept it if she took it at face value. She would go along for the ride, but no further. She mustn't start yearning for things Rafe Carter was never going to give her. Because even though he'd taken her to heaven and back last night, this morning his eyes were cold and unwelcoming.

He doesn't much like you either, she thought.

And even though his opinion didn't matter, wasn't it funny how something like that could hurt?

CHAPTER FIVE

FORTY THOUSAND FEET above the South China Sea and wanting to break the hours of interminable silence, Sophie turned towards the brooding figure who was seated beside her. 'I'm surprised you don't have bodyguards.'

Rafe looked up from the papers he'd been reading, his eyes narrowing, clearly irritated at having been interrupted from the work which had consumed his attention since they'd first boarded the aircraft. 'Why the hell should I have bodyguards?'

Sophie waved a hand to encompass all the luxurious fittings of his private jet. 'Why not? You travel like a royal. You're rich as Croesus. Aren't you worried that somebody might kidnap you and spirit away your vast fortune?'

His grey eyes glittered. 'I have a black belt in

both karate and judo,' he said silkily. 'I'd like to see somebody try.'

Sophie absorbed this as he picked up his papers again and she stared at the white clouds billowing outside the aircraft window. Her comparison hadn't been made lightly. Their journey from Poonbarra had been so smooth that at times it *had* felt like being part of a royal convoy again. Yet she'd been sad at having to say goodbye to the Outback station where everyone had just accepted her as she was. To them she was an ordinary woman who'd learnt how to cook and mop floors and use a dishwasher. She had been dreading the moment of confessing her identity to Andy and the other men, knowing it would change everything. But she had been wrong, because they'd acted as if it meant nothing. They'd gruffly told her they wished she weren't going. And hadn't tears pricked at the corners of her eyes as the car had left Poonbarra for ever, her feeling as though she was leaving behind a peace and a freedom she would never know again?

They had flown in a light aircraft to Brisbane

airport, where Rafe's private jet had been fuelled and ready to go. He'd made her telephone her brother and tell him that she was flying to England under his protection. And although Myron had been angry, his relief at being able to speak to her after so long, and knowing she was 'in safe hands', was almost palpable. And now they were flying towards the UK and it felt unreal. It *was* unreal. She was going to England to meet the family of a man who clearly couldn't stand her—and she didn't have a clue what she was going to do afterwards.

Her heart sank. Everything had been fine until he'd turned up at Poonbarra. She'd thought she'd have another couple of months before she needed to make any major decisions about her future, but Rafe Carter's seduction had changed everything. Should she ask him about flights to Isolaverde once the ceremony was over? She stared at his proud, carved profile. Maybe not right now. Why not prepare herself for what lay ahead instead?

She cleared her throat. 'Maybe you should tell me something about your family.'

He looked up, his face not particularly friendly. 'Like what?'

'A few facts would help. Who's going to be at this Christening. That sort of thing.'

Answering questions of a personal nature was an activity Rafe habitually avoided and, besides, he wasn't in the mood to talk to Sophie. He was still angry with her. For her deception. For not telling him who she really was. For coming onto him and failing to tell him she was a virgin.

Yet his body was refusing to listen to the disapproval which was clouding his mind. The single thought which consumed him was how much he wanted to have sex with her by daylight—with the sun streaming in through the cabin windows and illuminating her creamy body. His throat thickened as he imagined her arching that elegant back, those long legs stiffening helplessly as she came. He didn't usually bring lovers on long-haul flights because being trapped in an enclosed space for so many hours meant the possibility of boredom was very high. But for once there had been no other option.

Pushing his erotic thoughts away, he met the questioning look in her eyes.

'It's my nephew's christening,' he said shortly.

'Right,' she said. 'So is it your brother or your sister who is the parent?'

'My half-brother. Or at least, one of them.'

'Right. And how many half-brothers do you have?'

With a barely stifled sigh of irritation, Rafe put down his pen. 'Three. Or at least, three that I know about,' he answered. 'And a half-sister named Amber.'

'Gosh. That's a lot. How come?'

His instinct was to snap back: *how do you think?* Until he remembered that her privileged life had probably protected her from the worst excesses of relationships—of children born in and out of wedlock and illicit affairs which wrecked marriages.

'Because my father liked women. Ambrose Carter was something of a darling in his day, which is probably why he married four times and why I have so many half-siblings. There's Amber, Chase, Gianluca and Nick—he's the one who's just had the baby—or rather, his wife, Molly, did.'

'Are they're all going to be there?'

'Everyone except Chase. He's in South America, halfway up the Amazon. Molly's parents are both dead.' There was a split-second pause. 'But her twin sister is going to be there. Like I said, it's complicated.'

'Okay.' She shifted her gaze to his. 'And does your father—Ambrose—have a good relationship with his children?'

'As much as each mother would allow.' He gave a faint smile. 'Because a child's welfare is primarily down to the mother, isn't it? And the kind of woman who marries a man for the size of his wallet probably isn't going to be the kind of person who puts her child's welfare first.'

Sophie hesitated. 'And was…was your mother that kind of woman?'

'You could say that.' His laugh was bitter. 'My

mother was the kind of woman for whom the term gold-digger might have been invented.'

'I'm sorry.'

'Why be sorry? It's the hand I was dealt and I learned how to play it.'

'And was it...tough?'

For a moment he thought about ignoring her probing questions, until he reminded himself that he was over *this* stuff. He shrugged. 'A lot of her behaviour was thoughtless and I was left alone to fend for myself a lot of the time. But something like that is probably outside your level of understanding.'

'What do you mean?'

'Presumably you've always been protected from the more sordid side of life.'

Sophie hated his assumptions—the same ones people always made. As if the material wealth which accompanied a royal title made you immune to the pain and hurt every human being had to contend with. As if you lacked the imagination to realise what most people's lives were like. 'Yes, I'm just a poor little rich girl,' she said. 'Scratch my skin and I'll bleed oil.'

'If you're trying to play on my sympathy, Sophie, don't bother.'

'I doubt whether you've a sympathetic bone in your body,' she bit back. ' People think it's so easy, being a princess. That you swan around all day wearing a diamond crown.'

'Poor you,' he mocked.

She glared at him, wanting to make him see the reality, wanting him to *understand* instead of being so damned *judgemental*. 'Try to imagine never being able to go anywhere without people knowing who you are. Everyone listening to what you say so that they can tell their friends—or a reporter—what they thought you meant. Imagine people watching every move you make. Analysing you. Assessing you. Obsessing about your weight. Working out where you bought your outfit and how much it cost and deciding *that* colour makes you look washed out, or plain, or fat—and then writing a whole article about it. Imagine everyone knowing that you'd been saving yourself for your fairy-tale prince, only he decided at the last moment to have his fairy tale with someone else and their new baby.'

'I can imagine that must have been difficult,' he conceded.

She stared down at her bare hands, before lifting her gaze to his once more. 'Imagine suddenly realising that the sweet woman you bought a pair of earrings from is now using your photograph on her website to promote her brand.'

'Oh, I can imagine that pretty well,' he said, and suddenly his voice hardened. 'Somebody who wasn't everything they seemed. Ring any bells, Sophie?'

Sophie met the accusation which burned like hot steel from his eyes. 'I thought I explained why I didn't tell you who I am.'

'I'm just amazed that I fell for your story,' he said. 'Amazed I should have thought you were different from any other woman with your lies and subterfuge. And you aren't, are you? So maybe it's time I started treating you in the way I know women like to be treated...'

She didn't realise what he was going to do until he pulled her across the seat onto his lap and her eyes widened as she felt the hard throb of his erection pushing against his trousers.

'Rafe?' she breathed uncertainly.

'Do you like that?' he taunted.

She wanted to say no, but she couldn't—even though she didn't like the look in his eyes. But the hot rush of desire flooding through her body was powerful enough to make her forget about his anger and his mockery. All she wanted was to press her groin against that throbbing ridge of hardness which had brought her so much pleasure last night.

'Rafe,' she said again, her voice sounding thick as she struggled to get the word out.

'Shh. You don't have to say anything.'

Deliberately, he tilted his pelvis, so that she could feel his erection pushing against where she was hot and wet and aching, and Sophie's throat dried. It was scary and exciting all at the same time. It was making her aroused, but, more importantly, it was blotting out the pain of thinking

about Luc's new baby, which she *wasn't* over—
no matter how hard she tried to be.

'I'm still very angry with you, Sophie,' he said
softly. 'But that doesn't stop me wanting you.
Can you feel how much I want you?'

She swallowed. 'I…yes…'

'And you want me, don't you? Even though
you're trying very hard not to?'

Hating him for his perception, Sophie found
herself powerless to push him away. 'Yes,' she
said, between gritted teeth.

'Then we'd better do something about it, hadn't
we? And very quickly, I think.'

Now the excitement was unbearable. Sophie
felt honeyed heat rush to her groin—but social
conditioning went deep as he spread his fingers
over one aching breast. 'The…crew?'

'Don't worry your pretty head about the crew.
They're trained never to disturb me unless I call
them. Satisfied?' he questioned, rucking up her
T-shirt to reveal the cotton bra she'd bought
at the discount store, and Sophie gasped as he
cleaved his thumb across a nipple which was

straining frantically against the thin material. 'Because I'm sure as hell not.'

Insecurity made her say it, even as he impatiently tugged the T-shirt over her head and tossed it aside. 'I expect you do this kind of thing all the time? Make love on planes?'

His hand stopped from where it had been just about to undo her bra and his eyes darkened with an emotion which went deeper than desire. 'Don't ask,' he said. 'And don't project, because if you can't enjoy this for what it is, then it isn't going to happen. Understand?'

And suddenly she couldn't bear not to do it. Who *cared* how many women had come before her, or how many would inevitably follow? Why couldn't she just live in the moment and take what he was offering? And what he was offering was sex. Amazing and beautiful sex for the second time in her life. 'Yes,' she whispered. 'Yes.'

He didn't say anything more, just reached down to unfasten the button of her jeans before sliding the zip down and dipping his hand beneath the elasticated edge of her panties. His middle finger tangled luxuriously in the soft fuzz of hair there, before beginning to stroke rhythmically at her slick, wet flesh and she couldn't stop the small yelp of pleasure she gave.

'No!' Frustratingly, his fingers stilled. 'I choose my staff for their discretion, but I have no desire to provide a floorshow by having you moan out loud when I make you come,' he ground out. 'So either you enjoy this in silence or we're both going to have a very frustrating journey ahead of us.'

His clipped words were so outrageous that Sophie was tempted to tell him to forget the whole idea, but the sensation of his fingers against her aroused flesh was much more tempting and suddenly the last of her pride shrivelled beneath the heat of her desire. Did he sense her capitulation? Was that why, with a sensual dexterity which dazed her in every which way, he laid her down on the floor of the aircraft and tugged her panties and jeans down to her ankles. She waited for him to tug them off but he shook his head and answered her unspoken question.

'No. The jeans stay. You'll be able to spread your legs for me, but only so far. It'll make you feel...*wicked*, which is exactly how I'm feeling right now.' He unzipped himself and pulled his trousers down, his erection springing free as he lowered himself down to position himself between her restricted legs. 'You need to try dirty sex—'

'D-dirty sex?'

'Mmm.' He stroked on a condom. 'Surreptitious, partially clothed and very...' he thrust into her suddenly '...*urgent.*'

He powered deep inside her and Sophie gripped onto his broad shoulders as her body began to accommodate his stroke. *He was still almost fully clothed,* she thought, yet somehow that only added to her mounting excitement. Some of what she was experiencing was the same as last night—that blood-racing exhilaration and rapid acceleration of pleasure—but some of it was radically different. And he was right. The fact that her jeans were restricting her movements only added to the excitement of what was happening. She was his prisoner, she thought weakly. His willing prisoner.

She lifted her face, her lips seeking his, eager for a kiss which would blot out the urgent cries which wanted to bubble up from her throat. But there were other reasons for wanting to kiss him. She liked the way his lips made her feel. Because even if it was nothing but an illusion, they made her feel cosseted. But it was too late for kisses because suddenly her body began to spasm and just as suddenly he began to buck inside her with a ragged groan of his own, as he made those last few, final thrusts.

She waited for him to say something which might imply an ending of the undoubted hostilities which were still shimmering between them. Something to acknowledge that what had just happened had been beyond fantastic. *Again.* He'd told her she didn't have the experience to know that the sex was amazing, but she could just about work out for herself that it was.

'Better go and freshen up,' he suggested softly,

giving her bare bottom a light tap. 'And then I'll ring for some coffee.

Her heart contracted with disappointment at his careless reaction but she made sure she didn't show it, silently picking up her rucksack and carrying it to one of the bathrooms at the far end of the cabin. She emerged some time later, with her hair neatly brushed and a clean T-shirt tucked into her jeans, but the cursory gaze he flicked over her wasn't particularly warm.

'You're going to need something to wear for the ceremony,' he said. 'I don't suppose you've got anything suitable in your rucksack?'

'Not a thing, I'm afraid.' She forced a smile, wishing he would at least *acknowledge* the intimacy they'd just shared, instead of staring at her so coolly. 'I left all my silks and satins behind at the palace.'

Rafe nodded as he reached for the phone. 'In that case I'll contact one of my assistants and arrange to have some suitable clothes brought to the aircraft when we land.' He paused. 'And in the meantime, perhaps you could find something to amuse yourself with for the rest of the flight. Something which doesn't involve looking at me alluringly with those big blue eyes and asking personal questions. Because I have work to do and you're distracting me, Sophie.'

CHAPTER SIX

THEY ARRIVED AT just past midnight when huge white flakes were tumbling from the night sky as if someone were having a celestial pillow fight. Rafe's limousine negotiated the final bend of the narrow road and it began to inch its way up the long drive towards his brother's Cotswold mansion.

Sophie peered out of the window at the nighttime English countryside, thinking that if circumstances were different she might have enjoyed the snowy beauty of rural England—especially in contrast to the beating heat of Australia. But for now she was just grateful for the fact that the big house was shrouded in darkness—the faint, fairy-lighted glow gleaming behind the glass over the front door indicating that everyone had gone to bed. Thank heavens. She

wasn't sure if she could face a reception com-
mittee and wondered if Rafe had arranged that
deliberately by insisting they stop at a small pub
for dinner on the way here. Perhaps he'd been
delaying the inevitable meeting with his family
because he didn't know how to introduce her. It
meant she'd eaten her first ever meal in a Brit-
ish pub, enjoying the shepherd's pie the landlord had recommended though less keen on the
warm beer Rafe had insisted she try.

In the back of the car were a large selection of
clothes which he'd ordered to be delivered to the
plane when they touched down in England—and
she was now wearing some of them. Gone were
the cheap jeans and T-shirt and in their place
was an exquisite cashmere dress, which clung
to every curve of her body, along with a pair of
beautiful leather boots. They were the kind of
clothes she was used to wearing, but along with
her sudden change of image came that familiar
sense of being *on show* again. She stared straight
ahead, realising how much she had enjoyed her

uncomplicated life of anonymity and realising it was about to come to an abrupt end.

'You okay?' Rafe questioned as the car slid to a halt in front of the house.

'Not really. I feel as nervous as hell,' she said truthfully.

'You?' In the shadowy light, his eyes narrowed. 'But you must have met hundreds of new people over the years.'

Probably thousands, she thought—but never like this. Meeting somebody's family on equal terms was something she'd never had to do before. Mostly people knew who she was and had prepared accordingly and everyone was always on their best behaviour when a princess was around. She stared out of the window again and it seemed that the sleeping house had been nothing but an illusion, because the moment their car swished to a snowy halt the front door opened and a woman appeared in the doorway as if she'd been listening out for them. Her greying hair matched a dress which was clearly a uniform and Sophie saw immediately what the glow behind the front door had been—a giant Christmas tree, dominating a vast and imposing wood-panelled hall.

Rafe smiled as the woman in the uniform stepped forward.

'Sophie, I'd like you to meet Bernadette, our housekeeper,' he said, 'who has been with different factions of this family for many years. And if she wasn't the soul of discretion, she could earn a living writing about the exploits of the infamous Carter family, couldn't you, Bernadette?'

'Sure, and who would want to read anything about you lot?' answered Bernadette, her accent warm and Irish. 'And aren't you forgetting your manners? Who's this beautiful young lady?'

Rafe introduced her simply as 'Sophie' and Bernadette seemed content with that. And at least Sophie was able to chat easily to the housekeeper. Six months ago and her observations would have been stiff and formal, but working at Poonbarra meant she could now identify with the housekeeper in a way which would have been unthinkable before. She had learnt how to mix with ordinary folk, she realised—and for that she must be grateful.

'Is everyone else here?' Rafe was asking.

'No. You're the first.' Bernadette closed the heavy oak door on the snowy night. 'Some of the others are flying in tomorrow. Your father's got the four-by-four so he'll be okay. And Sharla rang to say she's coming by helicopter, so she'll be here about midday.'

Sharla.

It was an unfamiliar name which sounded vaguely familiar, but Sophie's interest was heightened by the sudden tension which had made Rafe's body stiffen. She glanced up to see a hardness distorting his taut features—and a darkening look which made him seem like a stranger.

But he *is* a stranger, she reminded herself fiercely. *You don't really know anything about him.* All they'd done had been to fall into bed where he'd made her feel stuff she hadn't thought she was capable of. *Made her long for things which were way out of her reach.*

A sense of unease whispered over her but she said nothing as they were shown up a grand staircase into an enormous bedroom, dominated by a king-size bed covered with a brocade throw in deep shades of claret and gold. Beside the bed, crimson roses glowed in a bronze bowl and, against huge windows, velvet curtains were drawn to blot out the snowy night. A huge crackling fire had been lit in the grate, scenting the air with the crackle of applewood, and the glitter of the flames was reflected in the overhead chandelier. The overall effect was almost medieval and Sophie unbuttoned her new coat and hung it up in the old-fashioned wardrobe before slowly turning round.

'Who's Sharla?' she questioned.

Rafe was reading something on his cell-phone and didn't look up as he answered. 'You've probably heard of her. She used to be a model.'

Wondering if his reply had been deliberately casual, Sophie nodded as she realised why she'd half recognised the name. Of course. How could she have overlooked that rare level of fame achieved when somebody was known simply by their first name? 'You mean *the* Sharla?' she questioned. 'The supermodel with the endless legs—the one who's married to the rock star?'

'That's the one.' He looked up then and the expression in his grey eyes was curiously flat. 'And just for the record, she isn't married to him any more.'

'Right.' She looked at him. 'But why is she here? I thought you said it was just family. A low-key affair.'

'She *is* family.' There was a pause. 'I told you. She's my sister-in-law Molly's twin, although I don't tend to think of her as family.'

She wondered how he *did* think of her. Why a sudden harshness had distorted his voice and why he'd tensed when Bernadette had mentioned the supermodel's name. But it was none of her business. She was here because they were supposedly doing each other a favour. And yes, they'd had sex on the plane, but that didn't mean anything—he couldn't have made that more apparent if he'd tried. He hadn't exactly pushed her away afterwards but he might as well have done. His attitude had been cool and distant. *Careless* might be the best way to describe it, as he'd tapped her bottom in that rather insulting way—which hadn't stopped her wanting his fingers to linger there a little longer. So did sexual intimacy give her the right to quiz him about his thoughts or his feelings? It did not.

She peeped out behind one of the heavy velvet drapes. The snow was coming down hard now—great drifts swirling down and covering the ground by the second. Rafe switched on one of the bedside lamps and the rich brocade of the counterpane was illuminated by a golden glow. Yet Sophie felt awkward as she watched him moving around the elegant room. He looked so far away, she thought. Any closeness they had shared now seemed to have been forgotten. He hadn't touched her once in the car and now she was supposed to be sharing a room and a bed with him and she didn't have a clue how that was going to work. How any of this was going to work. What did other women usually do in

this kind of situation? But she had wanted normality, hadn't she? Maybe now was the time to
embrace it.

Pulling the band from her hair, she shook her
ponytail free. 'What have you told them about
me?'

'Nothing. I told my brother I was bringing
someone, but that's all. They can find out who
you are when they meet you.' His eyes gleamed.
'Given your great love of understatement, I
thought you'd prefer no forewarning.'

'And they won't think it's odd that you've
turned up with a runaway princess?'

He gave the ghost of a smile. 'I come from an
unusual family, Sophie. Where the odd is com-
monplace and people break the rules all the time.
They might remark on it but they certainly won't
have their heads turned by it. And don't worry—
people won't bother you or ask you predictable
questions, if that's what you're concerned about.
Now,' he added softly. 'It's late. Aren't you going
to get ready for bed?'

His words sounded scarily informal, which

seemed crazy when she remembered being pinned to the floor of the plane, her jeans trapped around her ankles. But that didn't prevent a sudden flash of nervousness as Sophie grabbed her wash bag and went into the bathroom. The clothes which Rafe had ordered to be delivered to the plane contained nothing as warm or practical as a nightshirt—but there was no way she was walking back out there naked. So she kept her knickers on and pulled a T-shirt over her head. Rafe's eyebrows rose when she returned and climbed quickly into bed, though he said nothing as he went into the bathroom himself.

She switched off the bedside lamp and lay shivering beneath the duvet, listening to the sounds of taps being run and teeth obviously being brushed. The minutes ticked by excruciatingly slowly before the bathroom light was eventually turned off and Rafe came back into the bedroom. But it was long enough for her to see that he had no similar qualms about nudity and the image of his powerful naked body seemed to burn itself indelibly onto the backs of her eyes.

His words filtered through the air towards her. 'Why are you hiding away in the darkness?'

'I'm not hiding.'

'Really?' A hint of amusement touched his voice. 'Are you suddenly turning shy on me, Sophie?'

'Of course not.' How could she tell him that this felt...*weird*? That she didn't want to leave the light on because she didn't know what to say or what to do. She wondered what had happened to the woman who'd been so uninhibited on the plane. Why she'd suddenly morphed into someone who was feeling swamped by hazy fears. The bed dipped beneath his weight and she held her breath as she heard the rustle of bedclothes.

'Maybe you're jet-lagged?' he suggested.

'I think I am, a little,' she said hopefully, because surely sleep would blot out the tension which was growing by the second and making even the tiniest sound seem amplified. Surely the best thing would be to close her eyes and pray for oblivion to come, so she could wake up in the morning refreshed and able to cope with what lay ahead.

But sleep didn't come. She lay there stiff and unmoving, terrified to move in case she rolled against his hard, warm body—wondering how she was going to get through a whole night like this—when a soft laugh punctured the semi-silence.

'I know you're not asleep.'

'How?' she questioned indignantly, before realising that her answer had given the game away.

'Because you're trying to make your breathing sound regular and shallow and people don't really breathe like that when they're asleep.'

'I suppose you're an expert on women's breathing habits in bed?'

'I do have some experience.'

'I'll bet you do.'

And then his hand slid around her waist and Sophie froze.

'Just relax,' he said softly, as he cupped her breast with his other hand. 'Lie back and think of Isolaverde.'

And unexpectedly, Sophie started to giggle. 'You're…*oh*!' His thumb grazed across her nipple and she swallowed. 'You're outrageous.'

'So they tell me. Now, isn't that better?' he said as his hand slid down over her belly, and then down further still. 'Why are you wearing knickers in bed? They're going to have to come off.'

'Rafe,' she said thickly.

'Shh. What did I just tell you?'

'I…d-don't remember.'

'Then try.'

He slithered the panties down over her thighs and, with his foot, kicked them away from her ankles. But he left the T-shirt on as his fingers returned to burrow in the tangle of hair at her groin before slipping down to find her molten heat. Now the only sound in the room was the increasing rise of her unsteady breathing. He didn't say a single word, just continued to touch her with a lightness and delicacy which was sending her out of her mind.

'Rafe,' she said again, only now an urgent desperation was making her voice crack.

'What?'

'I…*oh*!' Her nails dug into his shoulders. 'Oh, oh, *oh*!'

Her hips arching upwards, her body jerked with helpless spasms as he lowered his head to kiss her. She felt the honeyed rush of heat as reality splintered into countless unbearably bright pieces and then dissolved into a dreamy daze. Afterwards she lay there, sucking ragged breaths of air back into her lungs. She felt lazy. Luxurious. Heavy and wonderful—but as her eyelids began to grow weighty, some nagging notion of inequality made her stir. Peeling her lips away from where they were glued to his bare shoulder, she touched her fingertips to the rough rasp of growth at his jaw.

'You must show me how to…' She hesitated, too shy to say the words. Or maybe it was because she didn't know *how* to say the words, and maybe he guessed that.

'Pleasure me?'

She licked her dry lips. 'Yes.'

'Go to sleep, Sophie.' He sounded almost *kind*

as he brushed away the lock of hair which had fallen over her cheek and dropped the briefest of kisses onto her nose. 'Just go to sleep.'

CHAPTER SEVEN

WHEN RAFE WOKE next morning it took him a minute to work out where he was—a habitual dilemma for someone who travelled the globe as frequently as he did. But usually he liked that sense of uncertainty. Transitory was his default setting. Most people were fearful of change but he wasn't one of them. It was the only thing he'd ever known.

He hadn't been lying when he'd dismissed Sophie's sympathetic words after he'd told her what a gold-digger his mother had been. It didn't hurt. How could something hurt if you had nothing to compare it with? Just as it didn't hurt that he'd always been pushed aside whenever the latest love interest had appeared in his glamorous parent's life. Why he'd spent school holidays in vast and empty hotel rooms, while his mother went out on the town. He'd learned to order room service and put himself to bed when there were no more cartoons on TV. He *had* learned to play the cards he'd been dealt and he'd done it by building a wall around his heart. At first the foundations had been rocky, because what did a small boy know about emotional protection and self-reliance, when it went against the natural order of things? But the more you did something, the better at it you got—and these days nothing touched him. His mouth hardened. *Nothing.*

He glanced around the bedroom, realising he was in his brother's Cotswold home. Only then did he acknowledge the warm and sated feeling which came after a night of particularly good sex. He turned his head to find Sophie's side of the bed empty.

Lazily he stretched, his body hardening as he listened for sounds of running water or any suggestion she might be tidying her hair in preparation for an early morning kiss, but there was nothing. He bashed one of the pillows with his fist and comfortably rearranged his head on it, thinking maybe it was better this way. Better than her snuggling up close trying to do that thing women always did after a night like that—stroking their finger in a slow circle over his belly and wondering what made him tick.

Because they had reached for each other in the darkness before dawn—caught in that strange half-world between waking and sleeping. Two naked bodies, doing what came naturally. He stared up at the ceiling—at the fractured light and shadows cast by the antique chandelier. Only it hadn't felt like that. Her skin had been silky-soft and her body as warm as soft candle wax you could mould with your fingers. She'd felt so tight when he entered her.

Briefly, he closed his eyes. Almost as tight as the first time. And she'd started saying things in Greek as she came. Soft things. Things he didn't understand but which instinctively made him wary—because when a woman starting talking in that tone of voice it usually meant trouble. He hoped her inexperience didn't mean she'd started to misinterpret the impact of a powerful series of orgasms. He hoped he wasn't going to have to make it clear that it was a waste of time for her to develop *feelings* for him.

Pushing back the rumpled bedcovers, he got out of bed and walked over to the window, blinking a little at the starkness of the tableau outside. He spent so little time in England these days that he'd forgotten how beautiful the countryside could look in thick snow. For a moment he stood, transfixed by a landscape which was almost unrecognisable—the long drive and other familiar landmarks obliterated by a thick blanket of white. It must have been coming down all night long—and it was still snowing, great flakes of the stuff hurtling down from the sky. It was the kind of white-out you usually only found in a ski resort and Rafe's eyes narrowed as he took in the heavy clouds overhead. It wasn't the best day for a christening, not by any stretch of the imagination.

Sophie hadn't returned by the time he'd showered and dressed and it was after ten when he headed downstairs, where he could hear the sound of voices coming from the direction of the dining room. He walked along the long corridor, unprepared for the sight which greeted him.

Because it was Sophie who was the centre of attention—and not because she was behaving in a princessy kind of way. On the contrary. She was sitting cross-legged on the floor right next to another big glittering Christmas tree, and she was playing with his nephew. Against the sparkle of tinsel and the gleam of fairy lights, she lifted the baby high in the air before bringing him down towards her, rubbing her nose against his tummy and making him gurgle with delight as she made a squelchy sound. And sitting watching them, with an overwhelming look of pride on her face, was the baby's mother, Molly.

Rafe wasn't expecting the painful shaft of ice which speared its way through his heart as he stood watching her play with the baby—he was outside the charmed circle but had no desire to enter it. But maybe his breathing had altered fractionally or maybe he moved, because both women turned round and saw him. He saw the uncertainty which crossed Sophie's face as she lowered the baby to rest against her shoulder, but her uncertainty was quickly forgotten as she fielded the playful swipe of a chubby fist as the baby urged her to play on.

'Rafe!' said Molly, getting to her feet and coming towards him with open arms and a wide smile on her face. 'Here you are. Awake at last! How lovely to see you. And Sophie seems to have made a huge fan of Oliver as you can see for yourself.' She tilted her head. 'But you really are naughty—why didn't you tell us who you were bringing?'

Rafe felt his body grow tense, but he kept his smile bland. 'Because Sophie prefers to keep her status low-key, don't you, Sophie?' He sent her a mocking glance as he gave his sister-in-law a hug. 'And besides, I can see she's made herself perfectly at home. She has a knack of doing that. Where's Nick?'

'Gone to speak to the vicar and to investigate how bad the roads are. Nobody else has arrived and they're all supposed to be here soon.' Molly scooped the baby from Sophie's arms. 'Here, let me take him and put him down for a quick nap before all the fun starts. You've been brilliant with him, Sophie—thanks.'

'You're welcome,' said Sophie. 'He's absolutely gorgeous.'

'I know he is—although I'm heavily biased, of course!' Molly gave a wide smile. 'I must say, it makes a nice change to meet one of Rafe's girl-friends—we only ever get to read about them in the papers.'

But Sophie became aware of the silence which fell like an axe between them the instant Molly carried the baby from the room. She met the silvery glint of Rafe's shadowed gaze, wonder-ing if she was imagining the unspoken under-currents which suddenly made the atmosphere seem so hostile.

'I like your sister-in-law,' she said.

'I'm sure she'd be delighted to have the royal seal of approval.' His voice grew rough. 'But you didn't think it might be wise to wait for me before coming down to breakfast?'

From the way he was glowering at her, Sophie felt as if she were in the dock. Yes, she probably should have waited so they could come down to breakfast together, but she'd *needed* to get away from him this morning. Needed to get her head straight and her senses back to something like normality. She'd been terrified of being caught staring dreamily at him when he opened his eyes, which had been what she'd wanted to do. She'd wanted to stare at him and stroke her fingertips over his skin and never stop, because what had happened during the night had thrilled and scared her in equal measure. The sex had been...

She swallowed. It had been *unbelievable.* Different from the first time and from the time on the plane. She hadn't known it could be like that. So dreamy. So close. Just as it was *supposed* to be...as if two people really had become one.

She remembered his arms wrapping around her and how unbearably excited she'd felt as he'd pulled her close. His kisses had been barely there at first—his mouth grazing over hers as if he had all the time in the world. As if he were exploring her in slow motion and bringing her to life—cell by delicious cell. And when at last he'd entered her, his penetration had been deep. So deep that she had gasped and murmured his name. But she'd murmured a lot of other stuff too, after he'd brought her to that seemingly endless orgasm which had left her feeling blindsided. Things she hadn't been planning to say but which had suddenly seemed to spring from her lips. Did he understand Greek? She sincerely hoped not. Or perhaps he did. Perhaps he'd guessed she'd been murmuring sweet nothings and that was why he was glaring at her in that accusatory way.

'I thought it might be easier if I introduced myself, rather than you having to explain it. Get the whole Princess thing out of the way.' She shrugged. 'I have to say that both Molly and your brother took it very much in their stride. And besides,' she added, when his expression still showed no sign of softening, 'I didn't want to disturb you. You were sleeping like a baby.'

'Really?' Dark brows arched upwards. 'You seem obsessed by babies.'

'I was playing with your nephew, Rafe,' she said, from between gritted teeth. 'That's what people do when they meet a baby for the first time. What am I supposed to have done which is so wrong?'

'Did you tell them why you were here?'

'Yes. I explained I was hiding from the press and you were helping me. Was that the right thing to say—or the wrong thing? Should I have run a list of correct responses before you? Perhaps you could have written me a few guidelines.'

But he was saved from having to answer by the return of Nick, his half-brother—who was brushing stray flakes of snow away from his face and hair.

Tall as Rafe and almost as eye-catching, Nick Carter had the same black hair and sculpted features as his brother. Sophie watched as the two men greeted each other.

'How are the roads?' Rafe asked.

'What roads? It's like a wasteland out there,' said Nick grimly. 'And I've just heard they've closed all the major airports.'

'You're kidding?'

'I wish I was. I haven't dared break the news to Molly.'

'Can't you postpone the service?'

'At this time of year? With non-stop carol services and a vicar who's run ragged?' Nick pulled a face. 'Fat chance. Which means most people aren't going to be able to get here in time. Just Dad and whoever his current squeeze is.'

'And Sharla, of course,' said Rafe, after a barely perceptible beat. 'She's coming by helicopter.'

Something in his tone alerted Sophie's senses again. Something which had started troubling her last night though she couldn't for the life of her work out what it was. *What wasn't he telling her? What was it about Sharla which was making him so edgy?* Or was she simply in danger of reading too much into a casual conversation because she wasn't used to being inside a private home like this? Sharla was probably as lovely as her twin sister—and Molly was a complete delight.

So she sat and chatted as Rafe ate buttered eggs and he and Nick drank their way through a pot of strong black coffee. And when Nick said he was going to speak to Molly, Rafe suggested to her that they go back upstairs. Sophie nodded, but her emotions were all over the place. He'd been very cool with her and she needed to remember that. To remind herself that he could be cold and curt, and it was only during sex that he seemed to show any emotion. But they weren't *real* emotions. She needed to remember that, too. Even she, with her laughable lack of experience, could work that one out.

Back in their room the bed had been made and a fresh fire lit in the grate. Someone had put a huge spray of seasonal holly in a jug on one of the window ledges—its spiky green leaves and scarlet berries contrasting with the dramatic whiteness of the snow outside. It looked beautiful, almost tranquil, but tranquil was the last thing Sophie was feeling as Rafe closed the door. She went straight over to the dressing table, sat down in front of the mirror and started to unpin her hair.

In the reflection of the glass, she saw him frown—as if her reaction wasn't what he'd been anticipating. He walked across the room and put his hands on her shoulders, starting to caress them in a way which instantly made her want to melt, but she forced herself to wriggle away.

'Don't,' she said.

'Really?'

She supposed it was an indication of his arrogance that the note of surprise in his voice sounded genuine. 'Yes, *really*.' Meeting his gaze in the mirror, she picked up the brush and began to attack her hair.

'You're bored with sex already?'

She gave a short laugh. 'Don't be disingenuous, Rafe. I'm sure there isn't a woman alive who wouldn't find you physically attractive but my emotions aren't something you can turn on and off, like a tap.'

'Why bring emotion into it?' he questioned carelessly.

'Well, what about simple manners, then?' She put the brush down and turned on him. 'You were cold and accusatory towards me downstairs, yet the minute we get back to the bedroom I'm supposed to fall straight into your arms?'

He seemed taken aback by her frankness. 'You seemed to be getting very cosy with my family.'

'So? Would you have preferred it if I'd been aloof? Don't you realise that's what people *expect* me to be? It was actually lovely to meet people who treated me normally. People I didn't have to put at ease, the way I usually do. Who didn't seem to *care* that I was a princess. What's your problem with that?'

'I just don't want them getting any false ideas about our relationship,' he growled.

'Oh, I wouldn't worry your head about that.' She gave a short laugh. 'I'm sure your attitude towards me will be enough to convince them that we have no lasting future. It's just a pity you're managing to ruin the present in the process. Great way to live your life.'

For a moment he stilled, as if he was going to object to her making such a personal comment, but he didn't. Instead his eyes narrowed. 'Is that what I'm doing?'

'Yes.' She could hear the powerful pounding of her heart as it slammed against her ribcage and knew she couldn't keep avoiding the question she was burning to ask. 'Tell me, do you and Sharla have some kind of history?'

There was a fraction of a pause.

'What makes you say that?'

'It was a simple question, Rafe. A yes or a no will do.'

Rafe heard the persistence in her voice as he looked into her luminous blue eyes. At those rosy lips, which were plump and parted. He could lie to her—of course he could. She'd told a few lies herself, hadn't she—so what would a few more matter? Except that their conversation on the plane had made him understand why she'd been so reluctant to reveal her iden-

tity. Even why her virginity had become a mill-
stone around her neck—something which had
been saved for a man who had ultimately chosen
someone else. Maybe there had been some *jus-
tification* for those lies she had woven, but the
same could not reasonably be said of him if he
chose not to answer her question directly.

And surely he could give her the bare facts. He
didn't have to give her chapter and verse.

'We were an item a long time ago.' He drew in
a deep breath. 'Over a decade ago, in fact, and
it lasted less than a year.'

'And did you—?'

'No, Sophie,' he said, because he was discovering that some things *could* still hurt, no matter how deeply you buried them. That when you
pulled them to the surface they could still seep
like a dark stain over your skin. Still make you
want to smash a frustrated fist against the nearest wall. 'That was a lot more than the yes or no
you initially demanded and it's all you're going
to get.'

He saw confusion on her face along with a

softness which affected him even though he didn't want it to. And although he knew he should resist touching her when she was trying to unpick him like this, something made him override his instincts. Was it comfort he sought, or oblivion? Reaching out, he pulled her to her feet and brought her up close against his body, his hands cupping her buttocks so that she could feel the hardness of his erection. And she did. He could tell from the sudden dilation of her eyes and he half expected her to object as he bent his head to kiss her. To pull away and demand to know more about Sharla, because curiosity was part of human nature and women were far more curious than men.

But she didn't. Was she intuitive enough to guess that right then he needed her kiss, in the way a starving man needed food? Was that why her lips parted, as if silently begging him to crush them with his own? And why, when he did, she kissed him back with a hunger which matched his, as if realising that in this, at least, they were properly equal? His tongue laced with hers and he could feel the urgent rush of blood to his groin as he skated his palm down over her hips. 'Sophie—'

'Shh,' she said urgently, pushing her breasts hard into his chest, her breath hot against his. 'Just do it.'

The unexpected earthiness of her response only fuelled his spiralling hunger and Rafe tugged the cardigan over her head, not bothering with the tiny buttons. Granted access to the silky camisole beneath, he rubbed his palm over her hardening nipple and felt her shiver as she began tugging urgently at his belt. His mouth dried. She might be a novice, but she certainly wasn't shy. He liked the murmuring sound of approval she gave as she tugged down the zip of his jeans and wrapped her hand around his rock-hard shaft. But when she started to slide her fingers up and down, he gave a swift shake of his head to stop her.

Picking her up, he carried her over to the bed, his hands unsteady as he laid her down and pulled off the rest of her clothes. Curve after silken curve was revealed and he resisted the urge to let his fingers linger and caress her until they were both naked and warm beneath the duvet. He wanted to put his head in between her legs but he wanted to be inside her even more. Somehow he found a condom and although she seemed eager to take responsibility for the task, he shook his head.

'No,' he said. 'Let me do it. I don't trust myself if you put your hands anywhere near me when I'm in this state.'

Moments later and she was giving an exultant gasp as he thrust deep into her moist heat and that wild little sound set off something deep inside him. It kick-started a level of lust which grew and grew, threatening to blow him away. He did it to her hard and then he did it to her slow. He licked her skin and sucked on her flesh. He was on the very edge of control as he cupped her buttocks and drove into her, deeper and deeper and deeper. He never wanted it to end and yet for once he found he couldn't hold back any longer. His body stilled for one exquisite split-second before finally he began to jerk inside her.

Eventually he turned his head and looked at her lying back against the pillows, her eyes closed. His voice sounded as if he was speaking from a long way away.

'Did you come?'

'Yes.' Her eyelids fluttered open and she smiled. 'Didn't you notice?'

Rafe stared up at the ceiling. Not really. It had been… He shook his head. He thought a burglar could have walked in and ransacked the room and he doubted he would have noticed. What was it about Sophie Doukas, this woman who'd had sex just a handful of times who could *bewitch* him like this? Lifting his forearm, he forced himself to glance at his wristwatch and to ignore the renewed lust which was hardening his groin again. He yawned. 'I ought to go and help my brother clear the snow from the paths.'

'Can I help?'

He turned to look at her, propped up on one

elbow, her glossy hair spilling down all over her bare shoulders and flushed face.

'You?' he said.

'Is that such an extraordinary proposition?'

'Are you serious?'

'Totally serious. What's the matter, Rafe—do you think the Princess isn't capable of hard, physical work?' Her blue eyes gleamed. 'I travelled halfway across the globe to get to Poonbarra. Even you were surprised that I'd sailed across the Pacific. Shifting a little snow will be child's play.'

CHAPTER EIGHT

IT WAS EASY to be nonchalant about your lover's ex-girlfriend when he had just given you the most amazing orgasm, but not quite so easy once that euphoric blitz of hormones had subsided and you were confronted with the reality. And the reality was sitting right in front of her in church—an ex-girlfriend known as one of the most beautiful women in the world, and Sophie could instantly see why.

She tried to focus her attention on baby Oliver, who was swathed in a shawl of cobwebby white, and not stare at the eye-catching vision who was drawing her gaze like a magnet, but it was proving impossible. She'd seen pictures of Sharla, of course—who hadn't? You didn't get to command thousands of dollars a day without having a high profile, but nothing could have prepared her for actually seeing the supermodel in the flesh. Sophie had met some beautiful women in her time—indeed, her brother had dated a seemingly endless stream of them—but Sharla was in a league of her own. Sophie found herself thinking how weird it was that twin sisters with identical colouring could look so different. Molly was exceptionally pretty, with her strawberry-blonde hair, pale skin and wide green eyes—but Sharla took those same characteristics and turned them into something quite breathtaking.

Maybe it was the high maintenance of her appearance which made her so mesmerising, because she looked as perfect and as glossy as an airbrushed magazine photo. Unlike Molly, Sharla's hair was shot with highlights of deep gold and rippled down to her waist. And unlike Molly, her endless legs were enhanced by a tiny pair of leather shorts and black thigh-length boots. This bizarre combination was topped with an iconic Chanel jacket and a kooky hat, which was an explosion of black and dark pink feathers. It should have looked ridiculous for a family christening in a small country church and in a way it did—yet the overall effect was one of beauty and originality. In her ice-blue cashmere jacket and skirt, Sophie felt strait-laced and conservative in comparison.

She risked a glance at Rafe but, judging from his cold expression, it was difficult to believe that a little while ago he'd been making love to her. Back then he had been animated and alive but he now seemed to have been carved from a block of dark and unforgiving stone. The ebony material of his overcoat hugged the broad width of his shoulders and echoed the blackness of his hair. There was stuff going on—she could tell. Stuff to do with Sharla. And much as she had been longing to ask more questions about the relationship he'd had with the supermodel, Sophie had bitten them back. She'd sensed he would tell her only as much as he wanted to. That she should be careful how far she pushed him because his defences were up and she wasn't sure why.

She had seen the unfathomable look Sharla

had slanted him when she'd sashayed into the fairy-tale church with its high grey walls and flagstone floors. Was that a normal look for a former lover to give? Sophie didn't know. Would she, one day—in the unlikely event of ever running into Rafe Carter again—give him a similar look?

Apart from the godparents, the only other guest who had made it through the snow in time for the ceremony was Rafe's father, Ambrose, a towering man with greying hair and piercing eyes, which were very like those of both his sons. Sophie felt as if she was being given a glimpse of what Rafe might look like one day and she was unprepared for the wistful way that made her feel. Afterwards, as they crunched their way over the salt-sprinkled path back to the house, Ambrose confided in her that he'd recently called off his engagement to a young yoga teacher.

'I'm sorry to hear that,' said Sophie cautiously, not quite sure about the protocol of discussing romance with your lover's father. And people randomly confiding in her like this was something else she'd never encountered either, since normally her status kept her well away from idle chatter. It was yet another thing she was getting used to, along with sex straight after breakfast and sharing a shower with a man when you were both damp with melted snow and red-cheeked with exertion.

'Yes,' said Ambrose thoughtfully. 'I decided maybe I should throw in the towel and admit that, after four failed attempts, I'm just not husband material. I always thought marriage avoidance was more Rafe's bag than mine, but maybe I was wrong.' He shot her a mischievous smile. 'He hasn't ever brought a woman to a family function before and I'd be lying if I said I wasn't impressed that he's turned up with a beautiful princess.'

Sophie knew this was her opportunity to make light of her relationship with Rafe and tell his father she was only there because of circumstance, but something stopped her. She told herself it was pointless to start a conversation which would only generate curiosity and more questions, but wasn't the truth rather different?

Wasn't she enjoying being Rafe's lover and revelling in the fantasy while it lasted? Why end it before she needed to?

So she offered Ambrose no explanation about her role in his son's life. She didn't tell him that she had put her decisions about the future on hold. She simply smiled and said how pretty the house looked. And it did. The two Christmas trees glittered with rainbow fairy lights and somebody had lit tall red candles, which flickered all along a wide mantelpiece decked with garlands of greenery. Old-fashioned carols sung by a visiting group of singers provided just the right amount of nostalgia and Sophie watched Bernadette serving drinks and food—along with some young girls who must have been drafted in from the village to help.

She thought about the total lack of formality which existed here, despite the fact that Nick Carter was obviously a hugely successful man. It was nothing like her own home life back in

Isolaverde. There was no procedure which had to be followed. No rigid timetable worked out to the nearest second. And best of all, she wasn't weighed down with the family jewels she was always expected to wear. She felt light. Free. Fulfilled. And more than a little wistful.

Her gaze strayed across the room to Rafe, thinking how gorgeous he looked as he stood next to the Christmas tree, deep in conversation with his father. She was doing her best not to think about the powerful body which lay beneath his charcoal suit. Just as she was trying not to constantly hover at his side, telling herself he wouldn't thank her for behaving like a *real* girlfriend. But once again she'd noticed the undeniable tension as Sharla had strutted up to him earlier, minus her hat and jacket, her perfectly toned arms glowing in the firelight. Whatever they'd said to one another had been brief but tense and there had been an angry glitter in the supermodel's eyes as she'd marched from the room afterwards, announcing that she needed to make a phone call.

Sophie saw Molly go over to Rafe and hold out his nephew towards him. But although Rafe gave an emphatic shake of his head, Molly wasn't having any of it and laughingly placed the baby in his arms. And it was as if someone had turned him to stone. The sudden tautness of his face and tension in his body sent a chill of apprehension down Sophie's spine. She looked at him uneasily. What was the *matter* with him? Did he really dislike babies so much that he couldn't even bear to hold one for a couple of minutes?

On the other side of the room, Rafe felt the baby wriggling against his chest and a dagger of pure pain lanced through his heart. His forehead was beaded with sweat and he felt an overwhelming desire to escape—even though on one level he could acknowledge the undeniable cuteness of his young nephew. But that didn't take away the complicated feelings of regret and guilt which still raged inside him. It was the reason why he never held babies. Because it hurt. Because it made him remember and think, *what if*? Because, because, because…

Did Oliver sense his tension? Was that why the infant suddenly screwed up his little face, as if he was about to cry?

'Bounce him up and down a bit,' advised Ambrose, and Rafe shot him a silent look over the top of Oliver's curly hair.

'What do you know about dealing with babies?' he questioned, as he tried to replicate what he'd seen Sophie doing that morning. 'You certainly weren't around for any of your own. Do you remember the time you turned up unexpectedly and Chase thought you were the postman?'

'I know. I know. I hold my hands up to all accusations of being a bad father,' said Ambrose, with a sigh. 'I married too young and too often and behaved like a fool. But at least you've taken your time choosing a wife, which might mean you've got a better chance than I had.' He looked across the room. 'And she's very beautiful.'

Rafe froze as the door swung open, and as Sharla reappeared he thought about the things she'd said to him earlier. 'Sharla?' he demanded, his mouth twisting.

'No, not Sharla.' Ambrose snorted. 'Sharla's like one of those hothouse plants you see— requires constant maintenance and remains as unpredictable as hell. I'm talking about your blue-eyed princess, who, for all her upbringing, seems surprisingly normal.'

Rafe opened his mouth to say that Sophie wasn't 'his' anything, but something stopped him. He certainly wasn't in any position to be able to offer any definitive judgement of the Princess, but privately he found himself agreeing with Ambrose. She *was* surprising, that was for sure, and not just because she hadn't pulled rank—not once. Or because she'd amazed them all by shovelling her way through an icy bank of snow, wearing some of Molly's old ski clothes and an unflattering woollen hat. Or even because she was fast proving the most enthusiastic lover he'd ever known as her acrobatic feats in the shower a while back had proved. One who had, despite her inexperience, chipped away at his habitual cynicism and reawakened a sexual appetite which had been in danger of becoming jaded.

Oliver began to wriggle in his arms and as Rafe lifted him up in the air again the baby gave a gurgle of pleasure. Grey eyes not unlike his own met his and Rafe felt a powerful pang of something inexplicable as he stared at the newest member of the Carter family.

'Ever thought about having children of your own?' questioned Ambrose, with a sideways look.

'No,' said Rafe as Oliver's chubby little fingers strayed towards his face, seemingly fascinated by the tiny cleft in his chin which all the Carter men carried.

'Or thought about who you're going to leave your fortune to if you don't have children of your own?' Ambrose continued.

Rafe stared down into the baby's trusting eyes, trying to ignore the sudden ache in his heart. 'There are countless charities who will be glad to benefit from my wealth.'

'But that isn't the same thing,' said Ambrose. 'Believe me when I tell you that it all boils down to flesh and blood. And that, in the end, nothing else matters.'

The sudden reedy quality in his father's voice made Rafe realise that the old man was thinking about the end of his own life and it was a sobering thought. He reflected on Ambrose's words during the champagne toast and the cutting of the cake afterwards. It had never particularly bothered him to think that he would not pass on his own genes, but suddenly a wave of emptiness and futility swept over him. Would he one day stand in a room like this, as his father was doing? Only the difference would be that he wouldn't have adult children of his own. He would be standing there protected by the icy shell he had constructed—a lonely old man with nobody to leave his vast fortune to.

The walls seemed to be closing in on him and he found himself walking across the room to where Sophie stood, chatting to one of the godparents. Sliding his arm round her waist, he manoeuvred her away from the conversation, wanting the oblivion-giving warmth of her body to chase away some of these damned demons.

'Come upstairs,' he said, his lips close against her scented hair.

She drew back, eyebrows raised. 'Won't people miss you?'

'Now.'

Sophie hesitated, thinking how autocratic he sounded—and wondering if he always got his own way. But why refuse to accompany him just to make a point? She'd had enough of meeting the occasional baleful stare from Sharla, even though the model had been nothing but steely politeness when they'd been introduced.

She didn't say another word until they were back in their room and she pulled the pashmina from her neck, letting it flutter into a pale blue heap on a nearby chair. 'So why the sudden masterful display of bringing me up here before the party's properly ended?' she questioned. 'Was that all for Sharla's benefit?'

'For Sharla's benefit?' He frowned. 'What's that supposed to mean?'

Sophie stared out of the window, at the black snake of the newly shovelled driveway she'd helped clear, before meeting Rafe's shuttered gaze. 'I don't have any ex-lovers to base my hunch on but I've been observing people for as long as I can remember.' She sucked in a deep breath. 'And for someone you split up with such a long time ago, there seemed a lot of underlying *stuff* going on between you both. What did she say to you downstairs?'

'That's none of your business.'

'I thought you might say that. What's the matter, Rafe—are you still in love with her?'

He clenched his fists. 'In love with Sharla?' he demanded hotly. 'Are you out of your mind?'

'What, then?' she persisted. 'Because there's *something* there.'

'Something? Yeah, you could say that.' He took a step towards her. 'You want to know what she said? Do you? Would it make you feel better if I told you that she made it very clear she'd like to be back in my bed again?'

She flinched. 'And that's all?'

How many more questions was she going to ask? Rafe wanted to tell her to mind her own damned business or maybe silence her with a kiss. But Ambrose's words and the memory of the baby who'd been wriggling in his arms had loosened the floodgates he'd kept in place for so long. Too long. He gave a bitter laugh as he removed his tie with a violent tug and slung it at a nearby chair. 'You want the truth about my relationship with her?'

He saw the faint concern which clouded her eyes before she nodded. 'Yes,' she said quietly. 'Yes, I think I do.'

She sank down on one of the armchairs by the blazing fire and looked up into his face. And although the idea of sharing confidences was alien to him, something told him he could trust Sophie. He sensed she could be properly discreet as her upbringing had taught her to be, but it was more than that. Something strong and sure was shining from her blue eyes to cut through his usual icy reserve. But as that reserve melted, he could feel the heaviness in his heart—so painful and tight in his chest that it was hurting him just to breathe. If he'd thought the years might have lessened the sorrow then he'd been wrong. So maybe it really *was* time he talked about it, instead of letting it gnaw away inside him, like some dark cancer.

He drew in a ragged breath. 'My brother Nick was going out with Molly for years before they married, and I first met Sharla at a party when we were in our early twenties. I'd left university and was a couple of years into my telecommunications business and she'd already done several magazine covers. My career was taking off and so was hers. In many ways it was a very satisfactory relationship.'

'Satisfactory?' she echoed cautiously. 'That's an odd word to use.'

'I can't think of a better one. I was young and horny and she was hot. I thought we were both giving the other what they most needed.'

'You mean sex?' she questioned baldly.

'I mean sex,' he echoed as he stared at her. 'Sorry if that offends your sensibilities, Sophie—but that's the truth.'

He watched her teeth digging into her bottom lip, as if she might be having second thoughts about hearing this, and maybe this was his opportunity to stop and change the subject. But he was on a roll now and the words were streaming out of that dark place inside him, where he'd buried them all those years ago. 'Right from the start I was honest with her. I said that if she was looking for permanence—for babies and wedding bells—then she should look elsewhere,' he said. 'We both had worlds to conquer and we were both so young. I remember she laughed when I told her the door was open any time she chose to walk away. But she didn't.'

There was silence as he stared at her, but she didn't break it—she just carried on looking at him with those bright blue eyes. And now the flood of dark memories were swamping him in a foul tide.

'One day she came to me and asked whether I'd ever consider changing my mind. Whether I thought I could love her or think about marrying her. To be honest, I was confused. I thought we understood one another. I asked why she was saying all this stuff and I remember the look on her face. The way she said, *A woman needs to know these things, Rafe.* And because I thought she was being practical and because I knew the rock star was pursuing her, I told her no, and that if she wanted commitment, she was free to go and find it with someone else. And then...'

His voice faltered. With shock? Or surprise? That he, who had always tried to distance himself from the conflict of relationships, had become an unwilling victim of one and as a consequence was plagued by a guilt and bitter regret which wouldn't seem to go away?

'What, Rafe?' she whispered, her soft voice carrying across the room towards him. 'What happened?'

He swallowed and it felt as if a ball of barbed wire were trying to force its way down his throat.

'She was carrying my baby,' he said. 'But she never told me that. She didn't give me the chance to change my mind, or come to some mutual agreement which would have worked for us all. I didn't know and I didn't find out. At least, not until afterwards, when she told me what she'd done.'

'Oh, no.' Her face blanched as the true meaning of his words sank in. 'Oh, Rafe.'

'Yes.' He looked at her quite calmly and then his voice broke. 'She killed my baby.'

Sophie's heart squeezed painfully as she heard the rawness in his voice and she wanted to jump up from the chair and wrap her arms tightly around him. To stroke his ravaged face with all the tenderness she possessed until some of his unbearable grief had subsided. But something held her back, some bone-deep instinct which told her to go easy around this damaged man. He had confided in her. Had told her the dark secret it was clear still haunted him. Wasn't it enough to be understanding and kind and calm? Not go over the top with an emotional response which would help no one, least of all him.

'I'm so sorry,' she whispered.

'Yeah. Me, too.' He swallowed before rasping out the next words. 'I would have supported her. Provided for her. Even married her. Done any damned thing she might reasonably have wanted. But I never got the chance.'

'Because you were powerless,' she said slowly. 'A man always is in a situation like that. She didn't want you to know and there was nothing else you could have done. You answered her questions truthfully because you didn't know why she was asking them.'

'And maybe I should have guessed,' he said bitterly.

'But you didn't have that kind of relationship, did you? It was supposed to be upfront and honest, but that only works if both parties want the same thing. Was that around the time you left England?'

He nodded. 'I couldn't wait to get away. To leave the old, tainted life behind me. I went to

Australia and started a new life there. I set up offices in Brisbane and bought the cattle station. I just happened to be in the right place at the right time—because the country was ripe for new technology. The money started pouring in and the work provided a distraction, but whenever I could I would spend any spare time I had at Poonbarra, working on the land.'

It must have been a kind of escape for him, thought Sophie, to muster those cattle and build those fences. To toil and sweat beneath the fierce and unforgiving sun. A new life, far away from the pain of the old one. Just as it had been for her.

She guessed that was why he'd rarely returned to England and why he hadn't seen much of his family over the years, because the chance of running into Molly's twin must have filled him with horror. She thought about what he'd said about his mother. Women hadn't done right by Rafe Carter, had they? No wonder he'd stayed away from commitment and why he regarded them as nothing more than sexual playthings.

But today he had confronted all the darkness of his past. Did that mean he had drawn a line in the sand and could finally leave it behind?

'Rafe—'

'No.' His voice was harsh now. 'I don't want to talk about it any more, Sophie. Do you understand?'

Oh, she understood, all right. How could she fail to? She nodded as he began to walk towards her and knew from the dark look on his face that he wanted to take out his pent-up anger and frustration on her and just how he intended to do it. Was he treating her as a convenience, using her to blot out the bitter memories of what another woman had done to him, and shouldn't she object to that? Yet the moment he pulled her into his arms and kissed her, she didn't care. Who cared if his passion was fuelled by anger? Was it so wrong to want him this badly?

She acknowledged the brutal hardness of his kiss, but when her hands reached up to cradle his head, he groaned and softened it. He unzipped her skirt so that it pooled around her ankles and she stepped out of it and pulled at his trouser belt, as intent on quickly removing his clothes as he was hers. But she could feel something deep in her heart being tugged as he drew her against his naked body. Some stupid little ache that made her long for something more than the satisfaction of the physical.

The rug in front of the blazing fire wasn't particularly soft but Sophie didn't care about that either. All she could feel was the warmth from the flames licking over their bare skin as their bodies met. Wordlessly she moved over him, straddling him. She could feel the hard bones of his hips against the softness of her thighs—and he felt very big as she brought him deep inside her. They'd never done it in this position before and her initial tentativeness was instantly banished by the smoky look of pleasure on his face as he filled her. He spread his fingers over her breasts and played with her hardened nipples as she rode him with a total lack of inhibition. And when her body began to tighten with the now familiar shimmerings of orgasm, his hands anchored her so that he went deeper still until she gasped out loud, in Greek.

She must have drifted off to sleep because when she opened her eyes, it was to find that Rafe had covered them with a blanket and his naked body was pressed against her bare back. For a moment she just revelled in the feel of his warm flesh next to hers and the way he'd slung his arm over her hips, so that his fingertips rested carelessly in the cluster of curls at her thighs. She remembered the things he'd told her about his past. The way he'd unburdened himself. Did it mean something that he'd chosen to confide in her, or was she in danger of reading too much into the situation? No matter. The future could wait. Lying there together like that was just about perfect and as she stirred a little she could feel his hand automatically begin to drift downwards, when there was a loud banging at the bedroom door.

'Rafe?' It was Nick's voice.

'Go away,' Rafe mumbled, his breath warm against the back of her neck.

'I need to speak to you. *Now.*'

Cursing a little beneath his breath, Rafe got to his feet and pulled on a pair of jeans, still doing up the zip as he walked over and opened the door, behind which his half-brother was standing. He didn't invite him in and Sophie couldn't hear what was being said—only the low murmur of their voices before Rafe quietly closed the door and came back into the room.

She looked up into his face, but if she'd been hoping for some new kind of openness after the things they'd talked about, then she'd been way off mark because his features were as dark and as unreadable as ever. 'Is something wrong?'

'You could say that.' His voice sounded grim. 'My brother's had a phone call from the landlord of the local pub. The snow has started to melt and a man and woman have checked in. He thinks they may be journalists.'

She sat up, clutching onto the blanket. 'How—?'

He shrugged. 'I suspect Sharla let them know you're here—inadvertently or not, I don't know. The question is how we deal with it.'

Sophie shook her head. 'There's only one way to deal with it and I can't keep avoiding it for ever. There's no point in me trying to concoct another life—it won't make any difference. And maybe it's time to stop running.' She clutched the blanket a little tighter to her breasts. 'To let Myron know I'm a grown-up now and can make my own decisions. To tell him that I need to forge a new future for myself.'

His eyes narrowed. 'And do you know what that future will be?'

'Not yet. I'd just hoped...'

'Hoped what?' he questioned as her words tailed away.

She shrugged. 'I don't know. After my fairly successful stab at independence, it's a pity I have to return being pursued by the press. I'd hoped to make a more...*controlled* arrival.'

'Unless you refuse to play ball,' he said slowly.

'What do you mean?'

'Why *should* the damned press back you into a corner?' he demanded. 'Why go back earlier than originally planned?'

'That was pretty much on the cards the minute you returned unexpectedly to Poonbarra. I don't really have any alternative, Rafe. I can't stay here. And I can't face the thought of turning up somewhere else just before Christmas, with a load of news-hungry journalists on my tail.'

There was a pause. 'Unless you came to New York with me for Christmas.'

Sophie tried to squash the leap of hope in her heart as she met his shadowed gaze. 'But you must have plans?'

'None I can't get out of. The only thing set in stone is my Boxing Day ski trip to Vermont. But New York is the most anonymous city in the world and I can have my PR people make sure nobody bothers you.'

'I don't know,' she said, even though she was filled with an excitement she was trying very hard to contain.

'The city is beautiful during the holidays,' he continued softly. 'And I think there's a lot more sex we need to have before I'm willing to let you go. I'm not offering you a home, Sophie—

as long as you understand that. Just a temporary shelter.'

Her smile didn't falter, even though the baldness of his statement left her in no doubt of his feelings for her. But surely it was better to know exactly where she stood. And he was offering her a solution, wasn't he? Practical help in the form of a Christmas break in a city she'd never visited, rather than a scandal-wrapped return to her island home. There was no contest, really.

'I'd like that,' she said.

'Good. In that case, I'll have my jet prepared.' His eyes gleamed as he unzipped his jeans and started walking towards her. 'And in the meantime…why don't you lose the blanket?'

CHAPTER NINE

THIS HIGH UP, the snowy winter light was on the harsher side of bright. A penthouse apartment high in the sky—far above the streets and away from the sounds of the New York traffic. Chosen specifically for its isolation and for the fact that nobody could see you, or hear you. An apartment Rafe had never shared with anyone.

Until now.

He stared at Sophie's back, silhouetted against the Manhattan skyline as she watched the ant-like people far below. His home, his space, his *life*. A fortress of a place which up until now had always been inviolate. People came here rarely because hospitality on home turf had never been his thing. He preferred to take people out to dinner, rather than be stuck with guests who wouldn't take the hint and go home. The same

with lovers, too. Not for him the awkward morning ritual of trying to remove a woman who
wanted to stay.

Why *had* he invited Sophie here? He ran his
gaze over the gleam of her bare legs. Because he
felt partly responsible for the arrival of the press
in the Cotswolds? Yes. And the sexual chemistry
between them had been an added incentive. Why
turn his back on a physical compatibility which
was as good as theirs? But it was more than
that. He'd confided in her. Told her stuff he'd
never told anyone else. Stuff which had stirred
up feelings inside him which had left a raw and
gaping void. He'd thought exposing his secrets
would make the darkness go away, but he had
been wrong. He told himself he just needed time.
And that maybe having Sophie here with him
was nothing but an insurance policy. A charm
offensive to get her onside and make sure she
kept those secrets close to her heart.

He acknowledged another stir of lust as she
shifted her weight from one leg to the other. This
morning she was wearing one of his shirts which

came to just below her bottom as she surveyed the cityscape. One hand was planted on her hips as she watched the snow tumbling towards the city streets. It was a pose designed to show off her long legs to their best advantage—something he suspected she knew very well, despite her relative inexperience. But she was a fast learner, he thought approvingly. She'd learnt to remove her clothes and tantalise him better than any of those high-class strippers he knew rich out-of-towners visited down on Midtown West.

His groin throbbed with a relentless beat as he walked over to her and slid his arms around her waist, lifting aside the still-damp curtain of dark hair to plant a lingering kiss at the base of her neck.

'Good swim?' he murmured.

'Fifty lengths—and all I had to do was take the elevator.'

'That's the beauty of having a pool in the basement.'

'Yes. Rafe,' she added indistinctly as he cupped his hands over her breasts and began to massage them through the cotton of her shirt. 'You do realise I'm standing in front of the window?'

'I do. And you're nineteen floors up.'

'Somebody might have a pair of binoculars.'

'The glass is mirror-coated,' he said, moving one hand down. 'Which means nobody gets to see—although, if it turns you on, you can always pretend someone is watching me slide my hand down between your legs and easing you open like this.'

'You are...' she gasped as he slipped his finger inside her '...incorrigible.'

'Am I?' He moved his finger against her, loving the way her head fell helplessly back against him, the scent of her sex heavy in the air as he brought her to a shuddering climax right where she stood. He felt the buckling of her knees as she slumped back against him and thought about carrying her over to the sofa. But she was nothing if not surprising because she quickly gained her equilibrium and turned around, her face flushed and a small smile on her lips as she ran the flat of her palm experimentally over his groin.

'Oh,' she said, digging her teeth into her bottom lip almost shyly as she explored the hard and throbbing ridge covered by the denim of his jeans. 'I see. You are a *very* excitable man, aren't you, Rafe Carter?'

He gave a low and exultant laugh. 'Is that what I am?'

'Among other things.'

The rasp of his zip sliding down was the only sound other than his ragged breathing as she sank to her knees in front of him and teased him with her fingers, before putting the moist tip against her lips.

'Sophie,' he groaned as her tongue gave a playful lick.

Sophie lowered her lips onto him, loving the sensation of sucking this most intimate part of him. She liked having the silken thickness of him deep in her mouth, just as she liked tasting that first salty bead of moisture which showed he was close to climax. He'd taught her so much.

About her body. About his. Sometimes she wished she could grab hold of time and freeze it because the clock was ticking down towards Christmas and once the holiday was over, she'd be far away from here. From him.

But her thoughts were forgotten as his hands clamped around her head and his fingers dug into her scalp as his excitement grew. She could feel him tense and hear that distinctive choking sound he made, just as he flooded her mouth and she drank him in.

She opened her eyes and looked up to find him staring at her and she slid her tongue slowly over her lips, which were still sticky with his salty essence. His eyes darkened but his hands were gentle as he pulled her to her feet and led her into the huge wet room adjoining his bedroom, where he turned on the warm jets of the shower.

'Where do you want to go for lunch?' he questioned, slicking thick soapy foam over her body.

'I'd love to go to that lovely restaurant in Gramercy again.'

'Then that's where we'll go.'

'Won't you need to book?'

His smile was wolfish as he sluiced suds from her skin, paying specially close attention to her thrusting nipples. 'I never need to book.'

Overlooking a snowy courtyard garden, the restaurant was exquisite and afterwards they went to an art gallery in Chelsea where a friend of Rafe's was exhibiting his sculptures. Sophie drank champagne and chatted with the artist and decided she liked New York, a city where it was possible to blend in and lose yourself. She liked it nearly as much as Poonbarra. Her heart missed a beat. The two places which had felt most like home had one thing in common.

Him.

She glanced across the gallery, where Rafe was standing studying a sculpture, his thumb rubbing thoughtfully at his chin while close by a striking-looking blonde in a mulberry-coloured velvet coat was trying to catch his eye.

Sophie thought about how it would be once she had returned to Isolaverde. That one day soon, this blonde—or someone like her—wouldn't just be chatting to Rafe about a marble figure, but would be accompanying him back to his gorgeous penthouse, to do to him what Sophie had been doing earlier. A sickening image sprang to her mind—of somebody else unzipping his jeans. Somebody else taking him so intimately into her mouth...

Sophie's heart clenched as she put her glass down on the tray of a passing waitress and waited for the feeling to pass. But these pangs of longing and possession had been getting more and more frequent as the days had ticked by. Was it sexual jealousy she was experiencing, or something else? Something she was too scared to acknowledge because it was as futile as expecting the sun to rise at midnight. That her feelings for Rafe were becoming more complicated than either of them would ever have anticipated.

Far more than he would ever have wanted.

She wondered if he'd noticed her attitude towards him softening, or whether she'd managed successfully to hide her growing feelings. She suspected he would push her away if he got an inkling she'd started to care for him in a way he had warned her against, right from the start.

She tried to pinpoint when her attitude had slid from lust into tenderness and then into a wistful longing for a future which could never be hers. Was it when he'd protected her from the press and continued to protect her, here in his adopted city? Or when he'd made love to her and shown her that sex could be about tenderness as well as hot, hard passion? She swallowed.

No. She knew exactly when it had been. When he'd opened up his heart and told her about the baby he'd lost and she'd seen the raw pain on his face and heard the bitter heartbreak in his voice. In that moment he had revealed a vulnerability she'd never associated with a man like him, and that had changed everything. And she didn't want it to change.

Because she couldn't afford to fall in love with Rafe Carter.

On Christmas morning, Sophie woke first—slipping from the bed and disappearing into one of

the dressing rooms before starting to busy herself in the kitchen. She gave a smile of satisfaction as she cracked the first eggshell against the
side of the bowl. Six months ago and she hadn't
known one end of a frying pan from the other
and now she made the best omelette in Manhattan. Well, that was what Rafe said. She was
humming beneath her breath when he came out
of the bedroom in just a pair of boxers, the hand
which had been raking back his mussed hair
suddenly stilling.

He ran his gaze over her. 'Sweet heaven.
What's this?'

She did a twirl. 'You don't like it?'

Rafe felt a shaft of lust arrowing down to his
groin. She was like every male fantasy come to
life and standing in front of him, wearing a short
baby-doll nightdress in scarlet silk, trimmed
with fake white fur. The tiny matching knickers—which showed as she moved—were the
same bright red and a Santa hat was crammed
down over her dark hair. 'Santa, baby,' he murmured. 'Come here.'

'It's my Christmas present to you,' she said, walking over to loop her arms around his neck. 'Because I couldn't think what else to get you. The man who has everything.'

'Best gift I've ever had,' he said unevenly. 'Which I'm now about to unwrap.'

The eggs were cold by the time they got around to eating them and afterwards they walked through the snow to Central Park, going by Grand Army Plaza and ending up in Bryant Park. Sophie's cheeks were glowing by the time they got back and Rafe made steak and salad. They ate their meal beside the tiny Christmas tree they'd put together with decorations bought from Bergdorf Goodman And when they'd cleared away the dishes, he handed her a curved package, wrapped in holly-covered paper.

'Happy Christmas, Sophie,' he said.

Her fingers were trembling as she opened it and, even though it was probably the most inexpensive gift she'd ever been given, she couldn't remember receiving anything which had given her quite so much pleasure. It was a snow globe.

A miniature version of the Rockefeller Christmas tree, which he'd taken her to see the moment his jet had touched down in the city. She shook it and the rainbow sparkle was momentarily obscured by the thick white swirl of flakes.

'Oh, Rafe,' she said, trying not to let emotion creep into her voice. 'It's…beautiful.'

'To remind you of New York,' he said. 'When you're back in Isolaverde.'

'Yes.'

The word fell between them like a heavy stone. What was it going to be like? she wondered and now the pain in her heart was very sharp. It wasn't settling back into life as a princess after all this that she was worried about—it was the thought of not having Rafe which was making her feel so utterly wretched. She tried to imagine waking up in the morning and him not there beside her and she thought how quickly you could get used to something, which had been the very best thing in your life.

'Have you considered what you're going to do?' His question cut into her troubled thoughts.

'Are you going to be content spending your days cutting ribbons and pulling curtains away from little bronze plaques?'

'No. I've realised that things are going to have to be different.' She forced herself to think about her royal life. A life which was a whole world away. 'I don't just want to be a royal clothes horse any more. I want to do more behind-the-scenes work with my charities, and I'm going to have to work out some kind of satisfactory role for myself.'

'That's the professional Sophie talking,' he said. 'But what about the personal one?'

She stared at him. 'What do you mean?'

'Isn't it obvious? Has what happened with Luc scarred you? Or do you want to meet someone one day and marry them, and have children of your own?'

She shifted her position on the sofa, flinching as if he had scraped his fingernails over an open wound. She realised that nobody had ever asked her such a bluntly personal question before because nobody would ever have dared. And somehow his words got to her. They made her want the impossible and the resulting pain was so deep that she spoke straight from the heart.

'Of course I want that. Most women do,' she admitted quietly, her cheeks colouring a little, because she realised there was only one man she wanted to do that with and he was right in front of her. 'But there are all kinds of obstacles to that happening so it's unlikely I'll ever get it.'

'What kind of obstacles?'

She chose her words carefully. 'Well, meeting a man is fraught with difficulties. It would really only work if I married someone suitable and the pool of eligible princes isn't exactly big.' She could feel her skin colouring as she stared at the tumbling snowflakes outside the window. 'Anyway, that's all in the future, which starts tomorrow. Because tomorrow's Boxing Day and while I'm heading for the Mediterranean, you'll be hurtling down the side of some snow-covered mountain in Vermont. Lucky you. You hadn't forgotten, had you?'

'No, I hadn't forgotten,' he said, turning her

face towards his so that his silver gaze was on a collision course with hers. 'But right now, the thought of skiing is less appealing than taking you back to bed for the rest of the day.'

'Making the most of the few hours we have left, you mean?' she questioned brightly.

'No. Not just that.'

His voice had hardened and Sophie screwed up her nose in confusion. 'What, then?'

Rafe shook his head. He'd tried to blot it out. To make like it didn't matter, but he was discovering that this new yearning deep inside him *did* matter. And maybe it would always matter unless he did something about it. *So do it. Do it now.* He cleared his throat. 'What if I came up with an alternative solution? Something which meant you wouldn't have to go back to your old life. A solution which might suit both our... *needs*?'

She stared at him. 'I don't understand.'

'Then hear me out.' He paused. 'I've been doing some thinking. In fact, a lot of thinking.

About something Ambrose said to me at the christening.'

He met the question in her blue eyes as the enormity of what he was about to do hit him and his heart clenched with something like pain as he realised he was on the verge of doing what he'd spent his life trying to avoid. But even the fear wasn't enough to stop him. He remembered holding his little nephew. The warmth and milky smell of him. The curly hair which had brushed against his cheek. Most of all, he remembered the sudden rush of yearning which had flooded through him and the realisation that having a child would be the only way he could heal the scars of his past. 'My father asked who I was going to leave my fortune to and I told him that I was planning for it to go to charity,' he said. 'But in that moment I realised that I wanted what I'd never had.'

'I don't understand,' she whispered.

There was another pause before he said it. Words he knew would create a line in the sand which he could never step back from.

'A family,' he said. 'A real family.'

She leaned forward, her hand reaching out to take one of his. 'Tell me,' she whispered.

And suddenly Rafe needed no prompting. He felt her fingers curling around his. Heard the loud beat of his heart. And the words just came tumbling out. 'Although come from a big family, I grew up not knowing my brothers or sister. My father kicked my mother out because of her behaviour and as a consequence, she and I were estranged from the rest of the Carter clan for years.'

'Because of her behaviour?'

His mouth twisted. 'Just how open-minded are you prepared to be, Sophie? How easily do you shock? My mother liked men. She liked them a lot. More than anything else.' There was a pause and his mouth flattened. 'Much more than me.'

'Oh, Rafe.'

He shook his head to silence her. 'After her divorce, she wasn't looking for a replacement husband because her divorce payment had set her up very nicely. Her idea of fun was having the freedom to ensnare some hot young lover.'

She nodded, as if she was absorbing his words. 'And what happened to you, while she was doing that?'

He shrugged. 'I used to sit alone in hotel suites,' he said. 'Watching as she appeared in the tightest dress she could get away with— usually with her second or third martini in her hand. Sometimes she would come back that night, but often she didn't rock up until the morning. I can't count the number of strange men I encountered the next day amid the empty champagne bottles and cigarette butts.' His words grew reflective. 'Most kids hate being sent away to boarding school, but you know something? I loved it because it was safe and ordered and structured. It was the holidays I dreaded.'

'Of course you did,' she said, her gaze meeting his. 'But why are you telling me all this?'

He didn't look away, just stared straight into her bright, blue eyes. 'Because when I held Nick and Molly's little boy in my arms, I realised what

I'd been missing. I realised I wanted what I'd never had. A family of my own.' His voice deepened. 'And I think I could have one with you.'

Sophie's heart began to pound, not sure whether to feel elated or confused. Dared she hope that *his* feelings had been changing, too? Was he hinting at the kind of future she had secretly started to wish for? Oh, please, she prayed. Please. 'Me?'

He nodded. 'Yes, you. You told me you'd like a family one day, well, so would I. You told me all the reasons that might not happen and I'm giving you all the reasons why it could. I can't offer you love, but maybe that isn't necessary since you are obviously a pragmatic woman. You told me you didn't love Luc but you obviously recognise that arranged marriages can and do work.'

'Did you say marriage?' she echoed cautiously.

'I did,' he agreed, and now his voice deepened. 'Because I can't see that it could happen any other way.'

'You would marry me simply to achieve your dream of having a family?'

'Your dream, too,' he pointed out. 'And no, not just that. There are plenty of other reasons why it could work. We are compatible in many ways, Sophie—you know we are.'

Sophie was so appalled by how badly wrong she'd got it. She'd been thinking about love and clearly he was focussed on sex. 'In bed, you mean?'

'Yes, in bed. I have never wanted a woman as much as I want you. I only have to look at you to…well, you know what happens to me when I look at you.' He smiled. 'But this is about more than sex. You don't bore me or rely on me to entertain you. And if you agree to marry me, I will promise to be faithful to you—of that I give you my vow. To be a good husband and a good father to our children. To support you in whatever you want to do.' His eyes were as bright as quicksilver as they burned into her. 'So what do you say? Will you be my wife, Sophie?'

It was a big question and Sophie knew the importance of taking your time with big questions, just as she knew you should never let your expression give away what was going on inside your head. She'd often thought a royal upbringing would have been great preparation for a career as a professional poker player and, although she'd never been remotely tempted by gambling, she was able to draw on those skills now.

So she hid her bitter disappointment that there had been no breakthrough in Rafe's emotions. Was she deluded enough to think he'd started to care for her, just because her own feelings had started to change? Hadn't he told her right from the start that he didn't *do* love? Now she knew more about him, she could see why. She could understand his trust issues and the reason why he'd never settled down. His childhood sounded grim and the cushion of his parents' wealth had probably made it worse. If he'd been abandoned by his mother and left to fend for himself in some grimy tenement block, the authorities would have stepped in and acted. But in the protected air-conditioned world of the luxury hotel suite, nobody would have even known.

And then there had been another betrayal—

an even greater one, by Sharla. Wouldn't a child of his own help him get over that terrible loss?

She looked into his grey eyes. He had vowed to be faithful and she believed him. He wouldn't do what Luc had done and lose his heart to someone else. During his own childhood, he'd seen the devastation that infidelity could wreak and he wouldn't want to replicate that. He'd never had a chance to create a family unit of his own and yet that was what he yearned for above all else. This powerful man with so much wealth at his disposal wanted nothing more than a baby.

And so did she.

His baby.

Why *shouldn't* an arranged marriage work? Some people considered romantic love to be an unrealistic ideal and maybe they were right. The marriage of her own parents had been arranged, and theirs had been a long and happy union. Why couldn't she have that with Rafe—and all the things which went with it? The companionship and the sex, and the feeling safe. Better no love than pretend love, surely? And sometimes love could grow...

She looked at him. 'But what would I do—as your wife?'

His grey eyes gleamed. 'You can do what the hell you want, Sophie. Just think about what you achieved on Poonbarra.'

'You mean I progressed from being unable to recognise a tin-opener to making a pie which apparently you described to Andy as "ordinary"?'

He laughed. 'He wasn't supposed to tell you that. I just don't like pie. But you're capable of anything you want to be.'

And it was that which swung it for Sophie. It was the same feeling which had come over her when she'd looked up at the stars, on that ocean-going yacht travelling out to Australia. That same sense of wonder and, yes...*hope*. It was the most empowering thing anyone had ever said to her and she could hear the ring of sincerity in his voice.

'Then yes, I'll marry you,' she said, in a low voice. 'And have a family with you and be faithful and true to you. Because I think you're right. I think we *are* compatible in many ways.'

He looked down into her face. 'We will make a good life together, Sophie,' he said. 'I promise you that.'

The effect of his smile made her emotions dip and wobble. And too much emotion was dangerous. She needed to remember that. This was only going to work if she kept it real. So she sucked in a deep breath and gave a cool smile. 'Yes, we will,' she said.

'Now, isn't it customary to seal an engagement with a kiss?' He pulled her into his arms, his mouth hovering close to hers. 'And then to buy a ring worthy of a princess?'

She brushed an admonitory finger over his lips, even though her body had begun to prickle with anticipation. 'Not quite so fast. The ring we can deal with but there's a protocol to marrying someone like me. Before we do anything, you're going to have to come to Isolaverde and ask my brother for his permission.'

CHAPTER TEN

SOPHIE'S HEART WAS racing as they were summoned into the throne room of the Isolaverdian palace. She could hear her high heels clipping over the polished marble floor, past all the beautiful oil paintings of her ancestors towards the dais at the far end.

It felt like forever since she'd last been here and the significance of the magnificent setting was never lost on her. It was where her brother had been crowned after the sudden death of their father and where their grief-stricken mother had sat, keeping vigil over the late King's coffin.

As she heard the heavy clang of the double doors slamming shut behind them, Sophie thought about everything she'd seen and done since she'd last seen her brother. California and an ocean crossing. The heat and dust of the Australian Outback, the silent snow of the Cotswolds and then the high-octane holiday glitter of New York. And now she was back on her island home, feeling a bit like a stranger on her home territory with the man beside her about to ask the King for her hand in marriage.

As they took their seats she wondered if Rafe was dazzled by the twin thrones before them— where diamonds, rubies and emeralds as big as gulls' eggs glittered in the winter sunshine. One throne sat empty—waiting for the wife her brother seemed so reluctant to find, for it was rumoured he had a mistress who was preventing him from fulfilling his destiny. Not for the first time, Sophie acknowledged the inequality of one rule for royal men and a different one for women. Myron had been allowed to have as much sex as he wanted, while she'd been supposed to save her virginity until her wedding night. How unfair was that? She moistened her lips with her tongue as she stared at the imposing figure of her brother, his dark face stern, his legs crossed with the carelessness of a man born to rule, as he leaned back against his throne.

'I understand that you have provided both sanctuary and protection for my sister,' said the King, without preamble. 'For which I owe you a great debt as well as my thanks, and for which you will be rewarded accordingly. The Princess has behaved in a way which was undoubtedly headstrong, but she is home now and everything is as it should be. Whether your desire is for land or capital, I shall endeavour to grant you your wish, Carter.' He gave a wry smile. 'Within reason, of course.'

Rafe smiled back. 'I'm very honoured to receive Your Majesty's offer,' he said diplomatically. 'But it was no hardship to give your sister my protection and, indeed, she fended for herself most admirably for many months. Months during which my men assured me she was the best cook they've ever had on the station.'

A glitter of irritation iced the King's blue eyes. 'I have no desire to imagine the Princess in a position of such servitude. Let us discuss how best you will be recompensed instead.'

'But, Your Majesty,' said Rafe silkily, 'I have no need or desire for any financial reward. I have no desire to accept payment for what was my pleasure.'

Nervously Sophie resisted the invitation to chew the inside of her mouth. Didn't Rafe realise that refusing Myron's offer was the last thing he should do if he wanted to keep him onside? That it was bad form to refuse the King *anything*?

Nothing was said for a moment as both men engaged in a silent battle of wills.

'As you wish,' said Myron eventually, unable to hide another flicker of irritation when it became clear Rafe had no intention of backing down. 'But on the other matter you brought to my attention when you first arrived, I'm afraid I cannot be quite so reasonable. You say you wish to marry my sister?' He raised his eyebrows before shaking his head. 'I'm afraid this will not be possible, for reasons I'm sure I don't need to spell out for you.'

Rafe nodded and then, very deliberately, reached out and put his hand over Sophie's. Had he done that to hide the sudden trembling of her fingers from her brother? she wondered.

'I completely understand your reservations, Your Majesty,' Rafe said. 'Because Sophie is your sister and you love her and care about her welfare and, obviously, I'm not the prospective husband you would have chosen—mainly, I suspect, because I am not royal. But I have a vast fortune at my disposal as well as the ways and the means to protect the Princess as she has always been protected. You need have no fears about her future.'

'That is not the point,' snapped Myron, uncrossing his legs and sitting up, ramrod-straight. 'I have had you investigated.'

'Of course you have,' put in Rafe calmly. 'I would have done exactly the same in your position.'

Myron's face darkened. 'And your family is… disreputable, to say the least.'

'We have a somewhat colourful history, that

I won't deny,' said Rafe wryly. 'But I won't do wrong by your sister and nothing you can say or do will change my determination. Because I intend to marry her, with or without your permission—although it would be better if we could do it with your blessing. Obviously.' His fingers tightened around Sophie's as he gave her hand a squeeze. 'Back in New York, I made a vow to the Princess that I would be faithful and true and I am repeating that vow today, in your presence. For I intend on being the best husband I can possibly be.'

Sophie felt quite faint. Nobody ever talked to Myron like that. *Nobody.* And nobody ever kept interrupting him that way either. She looked into her brother's face, expecting to see the first hint of the simmering rage which his courtiers knew to beware of, but to her astonishment there was nothing but a flicker of frustration in his eyes, which gradually became a gleam of reluctant acceptance.

'You are a strong man, Carter,' observed Myron slowly. 'And a woman needs a strong man. Very well. You have your permission to marry my sister. She will come to you with a generous dowry.'

'No.' Rafe's voice was firm. 'Sophie will bring to the marriage only what she wishes to bring. Some sentimental trinkets or the like, but nothing more than that.'

Some sentimental trinkets?

For the first time since she'd accepted his proposal, Sophie felt a shimmer of apprehension as Myron stepped down from his throne and she watched as the two men shook hands, almost as if they were sealing some kind of business deal. And the thought which had taken root in her head was now stubbornly refusing to shift, because wasn't that *exactly* what they were doing? The shimmer became a shiver. What she'd just witnessed had been a kind of battle between two very alpha men who were both used to getting their own way.

She realised now that if Rafe had backed down or buckled underneath the weight of her brother's arrogant royal power—or greedily accepted a reward—then the marriage would never have taken place. Somehow, Myron would have put a stop to it. He might have threatened to destroy Rafe's company or found an area of his life to target, an area which was ripe for exploitation. She would put nothing past him, for he had been furious when Prince Luciano had announced that he could no longer marry her. He had been angry on behalf of his jilted sister but there was no denying that he had seen the move as a slight to the royal house of Isolaverde.

But Rafe hadn't buckled. He had shown himself to be powerful and indomitable. He had stood up to Myron in a way she'd never seen anyone do before and he had won her, as a man might win a big prize at a game of cards.

Pressing her fingernails into the palms of her hands, she told herself to *stop wishing for the impossible*. To get real instead of trying to spoil her enjoyment before it had even started. Because this was what she wanted, wasn't it? She wanted Rafe—a man who made her feel alive. Who made her senses sing. Who made her think she was capable of *anything*. Hadn't he told her that, back in New York, and hadn't she been almost hugging herself with delight as they'd flown to her island home? And yes, there were limitations to the way he felt about her—he'd been completely upfront about that. He wasn't promising her love and fairy-tale stuff. He wasn't spinning lies and pretending to have feelings which were alien to him. And shouldn't she be *grateful* to him for that?

But as Myron stood up and prepared to take his leave of them Sophie was aware that gratitude was the very last thing on her mind.

'Thank you, Myron,' she said, aware that her voice was lacking the joy she'd expected to feel. All she could feel was a sudden and uncomfortable sensation of *flatness*.

'I have put Rafe in the Ambassadorial suite,' said Myron, his eyes glittering. 'Even though I understand you've been living together in New York, I suggest we don't bombard the palace staff with too many changes all at once. A commoner husband is going to take some getting used to and I think it's best you don't share a room until after your marriage. Let tradition reign supreme. I think we should adopt a softly-softly approach.'

Sophie glanced up at Rafe, expecting him to object to this as well. To a man with his healthy sexual appetite it would seem old-fashioned and hypocritical to be put in separate rooms. But to her astonishment, he simply nodded.

'That sounds perfectly agreeable,' he said.

'Good. And I should be honoured if you would be my guest at the New Year's Eve ball we hold here in the palace each year. It will be a good time to introduce you to the great and the good of Isolaverde. We can announce your engagement on New Year's Day.' Myron looked straight into Rafe's eyes. 'If that also meets with your approval?'

'Absolutely,' answered Rafe. 'I should be honoured.'

But as the King swept from the throne room Sophie couldn't shake off a distinct feeling of *disenchantment*—remembering the way the two men had talked about her as if she were nothing but an object to barter. Suddenly, it felt as if she had been slotted straight back into her familiar restricted role of *princess*. As if the stiff mantle of being a royal had settled over her shoulders and was threatening to stifle her. The woman who had shovelled show and beaten eggs while wearing a silly little Santa outfit now seemed as if she belonged to another life.

She accompanied Rafe and a small convoy of servants through the maze of palace corridors to the luxurious Ambassadorial suite and when they were alone at last, and the servants dismissed, he took her in his arms. It should have felt like heaven to be this close to him again, but Sophie couldn't shake off the notion that it just didn't *feel* right.

'Now,' he said, his thumb grazing over her breast and the warmth of his breath fanning her lips. 'What shall we do next? Any ideas?'

She swallowed. 'We'll have to get ready for dinner and my rooms are at the opposite end of the palace to yours, so I'd better... I'd better get going.'

'Dinner can wait,' he murmured as he ran his other hand down her spine to cup the curve of one buttock.

This was the point when she normally began to dissolve, when her blood would grow heated and her skin sensitive as she anticipated his love-making. But all Sophie could feel was an acute self-consciousness, the easy familiarity all but gone. She felt as if people were watching. Listening. Wondered if the servants were hovering in the vicinity, eager to know if the Princess was being intimate with the commoner she had brought into their midst. She froze. Rafe's fingers felt alien against her skin as he popped the buttons on her shirt and it flapped open. She felt as if this were all happening to someone else as he unclipped the front fastening of her bra and her breasts tumbled free.

'Dinner can't wait.' She swallowed as she stared down at his fingers—olive-dark against her paler skin as he stroked her breast—but for once her knees weren't growing weak and her nipples weren't tingling. For once she could feel *nothing*. 'That's something you'd better get used to,' she added. 'It is always served on the stroke of eight and to be late will be seen as an insult to the King.'

'So? That gives us a couple of hours.' He nuzzled her neck with a lazy kiss. 'Plenty of time for what I have in mind. I haven't made love to you in hours, Sophie—and I'm beginning to get withdrawal symptoms. But if you're telling me that we're on a tight schedule, then maybe we won't bother with bed. Maybe we'll do it… right here.'

She couldn't stop him. She told herself she didn't *want* to stop him and that much was true. Because she kept thinking that her familiar passion would return as his lovemaking progressed. So she let him push her up against the wall and slide her panties down over her thighs, and helped him as he carefully tugged the zip down over his straining erection. She even stroked on the condom just as he'd taught her to, but she didn't get her usual thrill of pleasure as he made that first stifled groan when he entered her.

She did everything she always did, wrapping her legs around his back, feeling the swing of her skirt against her naked thighs and burying her face in his neck as he thrust deep inside her. But today she couldn't free herself of a slight sense of *guilt*. She'd always seen herself as others saw her, because that was the way she'd been brought up.

Always be aware that someone could be watching you, Sophie, her mother used to say primly. *Because someone usually is.*

So that now, part of her was observing a princess pressed up against the wall with her panties down by her ankles, as Rafe thrust in and out of her.

She felt him begin to shudder and she whispered soft and muffled words in Greek to him. Words of excitement and encouragement and she kissed his lips hard and passionately when he came, hoping that would disguise her own lack of orgasm.

Neither of them spoke for a moment and when the last of his spasms had died away, she pulled out of his embrace. Awkwardly, she stooped to pick up her panties, her hair falling over her flushed face as she stepped into them again. 'I'd... I'd better go,' she said. 'And...settle in.'

'Sure.'

His face was curiously guarded as she put her bra and shirt back on and tidied up her hair, but he said nothing more as she left for her own section of the palace. And even the sight of her familiar rooms did little to soothe feelings which were ruffled by more than her scary lack of reaction to Rafe's lovemaking. Was her prolonged taste of freedom responsible for the sense of alienation she now felt in the environment she'd grown up in?

She looked at the canopied white bed, positioned beneath a soaring golden ceiling which had seemed so impossibly high when she was a little girl. She picked up a photo of her parents at a ball they'd attended before she was even born, her mother wearing the dazzling ruby and diamond necklace which Sophie had been destined to wear when she married Prince Luc. A necklace which now belonged to another woman...

Putting the photo back down, she showered Rafe's scent from her skin and then walked over to the wardrobe. The lavish clothes she found inside were worlds away from the cheap shorts and T-shirts she'd worn at Poonbarra, where she'd blended in and felt like everyone else. Running her fingertips over the soft fabrics, she put on a floaty dress of a blue so pale it was almost white, and went down to dinner.

The meal was held in the State banqueting room—a setting designed to show the palace at its most splendid. Old gold and cream roses were massed into glittering crystal vases and tall gold candles flickered all the way along the centre of the table. It felt like a jolt to be back amid all this lavish and very obvious luxury again and Sophie tried to shake off the feeling of being on show. She was next to Myron, who she could tell was making a big effort to be nice to her. She kept expecting him to berate her for her impetuosity in running away, but instead he asked her about life at Poonbarra—and it was all she could do to keep the wistfulness from her voice. And she detected an undeniable sense of *relief* in his attitude towards her. Was the King glad that his troublesome little sister was soon to be off his hands at last—passed from the care of one powerful man to another?

Rafe was seated next to Mary-Belle—with the Isolaverdian Prime Minister on the other side. Sophie watched as he charmed both her little sister and the high-ranking politician who had recently approved an extension to the country's world-famous oceanographic museum. Who knew Rafe was such an expert on marine science, or that he'd once scuba-dived in the Galapagos? She sat and listened as he made her sister giggle. Over the top of her golden goblet she saw him smile at something the premier had said and Sophie's heart began to pound beneath the delicate material of her silk-satin dress. He looked so gorgeous sitting there, but she thought he also seemed…distant. There were no meaningful looks slanted at her from across the wide expanse of the table. No suggestive smile. *And whose fault was that?* Had he noticed her lack of response earlier, or had he been so caught up in his own passion that he hadn't noticed? She wondered if she should have faked an orgasm, yet something deep inside her baulked at the thought of doing that—because wasn't this relationship of theirs supposed to be based on honesty?

Except it didn't feel so honest right then. It felt as if she was hiding stuff away from him. As if she knew it would appal him to realise the direction of some of her thoughts.

It was no better when the evening broke up and they were each assigned a servant to take them to their separate suites. Rafe gave her only the briefest of kisses before they parted—but what else could he do in front of all those silent, watching faces?

She slid between the cool sheets, wondering if he would steal through the vast palace to find her, so that they could try to make right that awkward one-sided coupling of earlier. She stared up at the ceiling, realising that this was the first night they'd spent apart since that moon-lit seduction in the swimming pool. Were these cold and gilded walls responsible for deadening her physical response to her lover, or was it that a lifetime of conditioning was hard to throw off overnight?

Eventually she fell into a fitful sleep, thinking about the sparkling engagement ring which Rafe would slide on her finger on the first day of the new year.

And she couldn't shake off the thought that it seemed all *wrong*.

CHAPTER ELEVEN

UNDER THE CURVING arches of a galleried ball-room an orchestra played and Rafe looked around him. Beneath the low murmur of voices, he could hear the occasional aristocratic laugh and bell-like sound of champagne glasses being chinked. Even for a man who had attended more than his fair share of dazzling occasions, the Isolaverdian New Year's ball was quite something.

He could sense people's eyes on him—at least, everyone's except Sophie's. She seemed to be avoiding his gaze as much as possible. He wondered if she was remembering that unsatisfactory episode of lovemaking yesterday, when she'd been about as responsive as a block of ice in his arms. His mouth flattened because that had never happened to him before—a woman staying ice-cool even while he was deep inside her body. And Sophie wasn't some random lover he could just forget about, or decide that maybe they weren't so compatible after all. He shook his head as someone offered him a glass of champagne. She was the woman he had vowed to make his wife and he knew it was a lifelong commitment.

A middle-aged blonde—a fortune in emeralds dazzling around her neck—was making no attempt to hide her interest and even though he was used to being stared at, it had never felt like this before. He was aware that his every movement was being observed, his every comment noted and analysed. Was this what being royal was all about—along with all the damned rules and endless protocol which seemed to make this palace seem like a giant institution? Was that the reason Sophie had been so uptight the moment she'd stepped back on familiar territory? Why she was scarcely recognisable as the warm woman he'd grown to know?

He glanced across the ballroom as she strayed into his line of vision. She was easily the most beautiful woman in the room, her dark hair studded with sapphires and a matching midnight-blue gown hugging her slim figure. But she looked cool and aloof as she greeted the high-born guests and once again that feeling of unease settled over him.

He had asked her to be his bride but he couldn't deny that doubts had started to creep into his mind since they'd arrived here in Isolaverde. Back in New York, it had all seemed ridiculously simple. He'd been on a high—amazed to find a woman whose company didn't irritate him and dazed from the non-stop and amazing sex. They'd each dragged out their demons and shone daylight on them and confronting them had seemed to diminish them. She'd told him she wanted a family and marriage; well, so did he. And the cherry on the cake as far as he was concerned was that neither of them was chasing after that disappointing fairy tale known as love.

But in the high-octane buzz of the city it had been easy to forget that Sophie was a royal, while here it had been in his face from the moment they'd touched down. And nothing was ever going to change that. He wanted children of his own—but hadn't he overlooked the fact that any child he sired with Sophie would be royal by birth? As soon as they were born, wouldn't expectation be heaped all over their innocent heads? Could he willingly subject any child of his to a life beneath the glare of the spotlight?

Sophie was walking towards him and he could see people bobbing into curtseys as she moved past. 'So. There you are,' she said.

'Here I am,' he agreed, his eyes capturing hers. 'And I'm all yours. Dance with me?'

She nodded, a small smile tugging at her lips as he took her into his arms and the orchestra swelled into a slow and sensuous waltz. He could smell a different scent on her skin, something warm and spicy, and he felt the punch of his heart as he drew her close.

'Having fun?' he questioned.

'Of course!' Her voice sounded bright. 'How about you?'

'This is certainly a very elaborate production,' he said dryly.

Now what did he mean by *that*? Sophie glanced up into Rafe's hard-boned face but his shuttered features gave her no clues. She thought how *unapproachable* he looked this evening, even though she kept trying to tell herself she was imagining it. But deep down she knew she wasn't. Things had been awkward between them since that disorientating episode of sex when she hadn't felt a thing. They hadn't discussed it because neither of them had acknowledged it— and hadn't she been secretly praying he might not have even noticed? That his own pleasure had been powerful enough for it to have passed him by? But the truth was that he hadn't laid a finger on her since.

Yet while his lack of attention had removed her fear of a repeat episode of unresponsiveness, it did nothing to lessen her dread about what was happening to them. Her growing fear that this was how it was going to be from now on. Her stomach tied itself up in knots as they moved around the dance floor. Because what if she was one of those women who couldn't sustain sexual enjoyment? She'd read about that kind of thing happening. Women whose senses shut down for whatever reason, leaving their highly sexed menfolk aching and frustrated.

And she wasn't stupid. There were plenty of reasons why a rift should have appeared between them and it wasn't just because they weren't having sex. She'd seen the expression on Rafe's face when he wasn't aware she was watching him. He reminded her of a person walking around a zoo and observing all the exhibits with a wry and faintly disbelieving look on his face. What if he'd changed his mind about wanting to marry her, now that he had seen her in her natural habitat of the royal palace?

She lifted her gaze towards his shadowed jaw and asked the question she had been dreading. 'You are still happy for the marriage announcement to be made tomorrow?'

The look he slanted down at her was unfathomable. 'I gave your brother my vow, didn't I? And I never go back on my word.'

But Sophie took little comfort from his response. Why, that was the most lacklustre endorsement she'd ever heard! The dance finished and an Isolaverdian nobleman she'd known since childhood stepped forward to take Rafe's place. With a smile, she shook her head, taking a glass of punch from the tray of a passing waitress instead. But she wanted a drink even less than she wanted a dance. It was more of a distraction—a stalling device—something which enabled her to observe Rafe as he headed over towards a nearby beauty to ask her to dance.

The beauty was a Duchess, an ethereal blonde who'd been sitting near Rafe at the pre-ball dinner, and she accepted his offer immediately. Sophie felt her heart plummet. Of course she did. What woman wouldn't want to be in the arms of Rafe Carter? Despite the fact that he had no royal title, he was easily the most attractive man in the crowded ballroom. She watched him move the Duchess round the floor, wondering if she was imagining that he seemed more relaxed than he'd been during his dance with *her*. But could she blame him? It couldn't be much fun dancing with a woman who had suddenly turned to ice in his arms.

She tried not to react but she couldn't seem to quash the sheer, blinding jealousy of seeing him so close to another woman. She told herself not to be so stupid—that it was all completely innocent. And it *was* innocent. Logically, she knew that. She believed in his vow of intended fidelity, just as she believed he was a man who wouldn't go back on his word.

But that was before she had shut down in his arms, wasn't it? Before he'd seen at close quarters just what it meant to marry into the pomp and ceremony of the Isolaverdian royal family.

Feeling as if someone were pressing their fingers against her throat, Sophie turned away and found herself a hiding place behind a tall marble pillar, dejection washing over her as she leaned back against the wall. Because nothing had changed, had it? Despite her daredevil stab at gaining some independence, everything was as it always had been. She had tied up her future with a man who'd promised her the security of marriage but without the cushion of love. Just as Luc had done.

And she was just as trapped as before!

Only this time it was worse.

Much worse.

She'd known all along that her feelings for Luc had been tepid, because they'd never been given the freedom to get to know each other properly. But she *did* know Rafe. More intimately than she'd known anyone. She'd been his lover. She'd shared his bed. She'd cooked him meals and vice versa and she'd lain face down on the pillows of his New York bed while he had carefully massaged her shoulders and then, afterwards, eased himself inside her aching body. He'd taken her to parties, and shows. They'd shopped together and walked for miles through the snowy streets of New York City. And if the truth were known, she'd fallen in love with him along the way, hadn't she?

Hadn't she?

The music changed to a lively foxtrot as she tried to tell herself she was panicking unnecessarily. That tomorrow Rafe would slide on the huge ruby and diamond ring they'd chosen together on Madison Avenue and the people of Isolaverde would be delighted that their princess had found her own happy ending at last.

But she hadn't, had she?

She was still that same dumb, docile princess who thought she couldn't exist without the patronage of a powerful man. She was about as modern as one of the ancient suits of armour which stood in the palace entrance hall! How could she knowingly walk into such a one-sided relationship and open herself up to all the potential pain of such a union? How could she force that on Rafe when the agreement had been that neither of them was asking for love?

Thought after disturbing thought rushed through her head, but she kept them hidden behind a careful smile as she went through the motions expected of her. She danced with the prime minister, with assorted Dukes and a visiting Sheikh. She even danced with Rafe again, trying not to indulge in a rush of jealous questions about his many dance partners.

And this was what her future would be like, she realised. Life with a man who couldn't love her. A man every woman would see and want and probably make a play for.

And she would be left watching from the sidelines, not daring to show him her feelings because they didn't have that kind of marriage.

'Relax,' he said, his thumb making idle little circles at her waist.

'I'm trying.'

'Then try a little harder.' He smiled. 'Because soon this will all be over.'

The decision she'd been trying her best to avoid could no longer be ignored and Sophie wondered if Rafe had any idea how eerily accurate his words were. Because suddenly she knew she couldn't keep running from the truth. Running only got you so far. Sooner or later you had to stop and face what was troubling you—and what was troubling her was that she couldn't let this fantasy marriage go ahead. For all their sakes, she needed to stop it. She swallowed. 'Rafe, I need to talk to you.'

'Then talk.'

'No. Not here. It's too public. Can we go somewhere more private? Please.' She hesitated. 'It's important.'

He loosened his hold on her fractionally, pulling back from her so that his silver-grey gaze clashed with hers. 'But the ball hasn't finished.'

It felt like a reprimand. It *was* a reprimand. How ironic that the commoner was giving the Princess a lesson in etiquette. 'After the fireworks and once my brother has left, can you meet me in the Ruby Drawing Room?' she questioned breathlessly. 'Do you know where that is?'

He nodded, but now his gaze was thoughtful as it rested on her. 'Sure.'

Somehow Sophie got through the remainder of the evening. At midnight the French windows were opened and everyone moved onto the terrace as bells peeled out all over the island to celebrate the coming of the new year. It was always an emotional time but tonight it seemed even more poignant as Sophie thought about what lay ahead. She could feel the prick of tears as the sky exploded in a spectacular display of fireworks—silver, gold, cobalt and pink flowering against an indigo backdrop— all reflected in the dark gleaming waters of the Mediterranean. She heard the collective gasps of the ball-goers echoing around the vast terrace as the fireworks whirred and whistled in the air, but somehow she didn't feel part of it.

And then the evening became nothing more than an endurance of clock-watching. All she wanted was for Myron to retire, because nobody was allowed to move until after the King had taken his leave. At last the King whispered into the ear of a stunning redhead before sweeping with his entourage from the room and, a few moments later, Sophie saw the woman follow him.

Sophie's heart was thumping as she made her way to the eastern side of the palace. The

Ruby Drawing Room was one of her favourite places in the palace, its décor overseen by her late mother, whose favourite colour and gemstone it had been. Hers, too. The walls and floor were in restful shades of darkest pink and only the ornate ceiling was gold—its intricate mouldings picked out with dazzling precision. It was a room which made her feel emotional for all kinds of reasons and therefore probably not the best choice for the kind of talk she and Rafe needed to have, but it was quiet and far away from the hustle and bustle of the ball.

She walked in and saw that Rafe was already there, tall and magnificent as he stood beside the marble fireplace, his grey eyes watchful as she pushed the door shut.

'So what's with all the cloak and dagger stuff?' he questioned.

She drew in a deep breath, her heart pounding with nerves. 'I've brought you here to tell you I can't marry you, Rafe.'

She searched his face for a trace of emotion. Something which might hint that her words had surprised him, even if they hadn't actually wounded him. But no. There was nothing. Those dark features remained impenetrable. And somehow that made her decision easier. It reinforced that she was doing the right thing—because he could turn it on and off like a tap, couldn't he? The man he'd been in New York seemed to have vanished. He seemed more of a stranger even than the day she'd first met him. 'I wanted to tell you tonight...' she stared into his eyes '...so we can stop the announcement being made.'

Not a trace of emotion showed on his face as he shot out the single word. 'Why?' And then his face darkened. 'Surely one episode of disappointing sex isn't enough to make you have cold feet?'

'It's a contributory factor, yes.'

He slanted her another unfathomable look. 'You want me to lock the door and make you come? Will that make you feel better?'

Sophie could feel her cheeks growing hot. 'No, of course not. It's about much more than that.'

'Like what?'

She bit her lip. She could do the easy thing of telling him she'd changed her mind and didn't want marriage after all. She could even pretend that she'd been sucked back into palace life and had decided that she liked it too much to ever leave. Except she suspected he was intuitive enough to know that wasn't the case—and besides, why on earth did she think any such option would be easy? None of this was ever going to be *easy*.

'Because we want different things.'

His brow darkened. 'I thought we'd already thrashed this out and decided that ultimately we wanted the same things. A family life together. Wasn't that what we both agreed, Sophie?'

And Sophie knew then that nothing would do except for the truth, no matter what the cost to her own pride. She kept her voice very low. 'I can't marry you, Rafe, because I've fallen in love with you. And I can see from your face how much that horrifies you.'

'Because love was never part of the deal,' he ground out.

'I realise that.' She licked her lips. 'Do you really think I want to feel this way? Because I don't—but I needed to be honest with you. I lied to you in the past about stuff and I think you realised I had reasons for keeping the truth hidden. But I don't ever want to do that again. And since our relationship is supposed to be based on truth then you need to hear it. And the truth is that I've fallen in love with you, Rafe. I've tried my best to stop myself but there doesn't seem to be a thing I can do about it.'

She stared straight into his face, willing him to say something, but she was met only with silence.

'Only something tells me that love won't work in a marriage which was only ever supposed to be practical,' she continued unsteadily. 'I thought… I thought I could do practical, but I was wrong. I'm not going to opt for second best. Call me stupid or unrealistic, but I'd rather hold out for love—even if that never happens.'

He nodded his head like a mathematics teacher who'd just been presented with a tricky equation and as Sophie waited, didn't part of her hope her words might have struck a chord, even if it was just a little one? That there might be a platform from which to springboard her growing feelings. What if he told her that he was receptive to the *idea* of love—would that be enough for them to go on? Wouldn't the tiniest crack in his armour mean that some of her love might be able to slip inside and warm him? She kept her eyes fixed on his face and watched as something in his expression changed. And it was as if the shutters had suddenly been lifted for there was no disguising the sudden hostility which gleamed so hard and silver from his eyes.

'I told you emphatically that I didn't do love,' he said. 'And you know why? Because it means nothing. *Nothing.* I've seen greed and lust and ambition, all masquerading as *love*. Did you really think that your words might bring about a fundamental change of heart, Sophie? That I was going to have a personality change just because you looked at me with those beautiful blue eyes and told me words I never wanted to hear?'

Sophie felt that little spark of hope crumble inside her, like a heap of dust onto which a heavy boot had just stamped. She wanted to break down. To sink to her knees and let the great slurry of dark emotions come sliding down onto her head. But she would not. She could not. She was going to walk away from this relationship with her heart shattered, but she would make sure that her dignity was kept intact.

'No, Rafe,' she said quietly. 'I didn't think that, although I'd be lying if I denied that's what I was hoping for. I thought you might be open-minded enough to the idea that feelings can sometimes grow if you let them—but maybe you won't let them. Or maybe you can't.' She met his stony gaze and nodded her head. 'We need to tell the King so that no announcement of our engagement will be made. We need to end it, as of now. Well, not tonight, obviously. But first thing tomorrow.'

'So I'm to go to your brother and tell him that my vow was worthless?'

'Oh, don't worry. I'll tell him. I'll make sure he knows that you didn't break your precious word and that the fault was all mine. I should… I should never have agreed to it.'

'Another marriage which has fallen by the wayside just before it reached the altar,' he observed. 'Are you really prepared to go through with the damage to your reputation, Sophie?'

'Better a brief spell of shattered pride than a lifetime of disillusion,' she flared back. 'Of always having to hide my feelings for fear that you might mistake them for *lust* or *greed* or *ambition*.' She swept the palm of her hand back over her chignon, checking that her appearance was pristine enough to face any servant she might encounter on the way back to her room, and then lifted her chin to direct one final look at him. 'Your words can sometimes be cruel, Rafe—but I suppose I should be grateful for your candour. Because, for the moment at least—I'm finding it very easy not to love you.'

CHAPTER TWELVE

HE HAD EVERYTHING he wanted. *Everything.* So why wasn't it enough?

Rafe paced the floor of his Manhattan apartment, where outside the glitter of skyscrapers meant you couldn't really see the darkness of the night sky. A bit like him. He was functioning as normal. Closing deals and starting new ones. Working out and going to parties. Life had to go on in every sense. He knew that. He'd even taken a woman to the theatre last night.

He stopped his relentless pacing and gave a ragged sigh. She must have thought he was crazy. Successful and beautiful, she'd made it plain she'd like nothing more than to have him share her bed.

And just the thought had left him cold. Worse

than cold. His skin had crawled at the thought of touching a woman. Any woman.

Except Sophie.

Damn her.

His pacing resumed. Why the hell couldn't he stop thinking about her, despite his conviction that this was the best thing for both of them? Because if he couldn't give her what she really wanted then neither of them would be satisfied.

An image of her face swam into his mind. Her eyes as blue as a Queensland sky. Her dark hair threaded with sapphires or tumbling free over bare shoulders. The cool smile she'd given him as he'd left Isolaverde. He'd thought the flatness in her eyes had been for the benefit of her watching brother, who was clearly irritated by this latest turn of events. But then Rafe realised it was all for him. There had been no reproach in her gaze—just a quiet dignity, which had preoccupied him all the way home to America and continued to preoccupy him.

So what was he going to do about it?

His mouth tightened.

He had a problem. Wasn't it about time he started seeking a solution?

Bright sunlight flooded into the breakfast room of the Isolaverdian palace and the King sat back and regarded his younger sister.

'I wondered if you might take a run out to Assimenios Beach today,' said Myron.

Sophie pushed away her half-eaten dish of grapefruit segments and forced a smile to her lips. The one which seemed to split her face in half but which she hoped Myron found convincing. He probably did. He wasn't exactly the kind of man who spent his life analysing the facial expressions of women, especially not those of his sister. Why should he care if she was happy or not?

'Any particular reason?' she questioned.

'Could be. I'm thinking of building a house there,' said Myron. 'And I'd like your input.'

'Mine?'

'Sure. Why not?'

Sophie opened her mouth to say she wasn't

sure her opinion was up to much at the moment, then quickly shut it again. Because wasn't this another sign that Myron was being more inclusive—something she had told him she wanted? It wasn't *his* fault that she wasn't firing on all cylinders, she thought as she went to her room and crammed on a light straw hat over her ponytailed hair. It wasn't anybody's fault except for...

She stared into the mirror, aware of the new definition of her cheekbones and the shadowed hollows of her eyes. She had to stop thinking this way. She couldn't blame Rafe. She really couldn't, because he'd been honest with her from the start. If there was any blame to be apportioned, she should heap it all on herself because *she* had been the one who had been unable to settle for what he was offering. *She* was the one who'd wanted more than he was capable of giving. He'd ruled out love from the start but she had demanded it—a bit like someone walking into a fish restaurant and demanding to know why there was no steak on the menu.

And it wasn't as if she were without choices.

She might have yet another failed love affair behind her, but things had changed. She was getting stronger by the day. Sometimes she even managed a whole fifteen minutes before Rafe's shuttered features would swim into her mind and she'd be reminded of everything she'd lost. No, not *lost*, she reminded herself fiercely. She hadn't lost something. She had walked away from something which would ultimately damage her and bring her pain—a one-sided marriage with a man incapable of love. She had been strong, not weak—and one day she would be grateful for that strength.

Just not today.

Myron had agreed to expand her royal role and to give her more responsibility. Just as he had agreed that if she wanted to go abroad and forge a career for herself, she would have his blessing. Because after Rafe had gone and she'd cried the last of those bitter tears, Sophie had realised she needed to take control of her own life and that running away to sail a boat over the Pacific wasn't the answer this time. She needed to stop letting herself be moved around by these powerful men, like a token on a gaming table. So she had gone to Myron and told him she was planning to enrol on a cookery course in Paris in late spring.

And Myron had just nodded his head and agreed!

Maybe independence had always been that simple, she mused as she climbed behind the wheel of her car, which had been brought round to the front of the palace by one of the servants. Maybe all she'd needed to do was to have stood up for what she wanted from the start. Trouble was that she hadn't really known what she wanted until she met Rafe, and now she was going to have to learn to want other things. Different things. Things which were nothing to do with him.

Reminding herself of his impenetrable eyes, she headed off on the coastal road towards the eastern side of the island. The sky was a shimmering bowl of palest blue, contrasting with the much deeper blue of the Mediterranean which glittered far below. The roadsides were thick with early spring flowers and the distinctive and unique yellow and white bloom known as the Isolaverdian Star shone out from the grassy verges as far as the eye could see. Sophie glanced into her rear mirror, the bodyguard's car further away than usual, thinking they were giving her a lot of leeway today.

Assimenios was the most picturesque spot on an island not exactly short of picturesque spots— a private beach of pure white sand, which was used only by the royal family and their guests. Crystal waters lapped against the sheltered bay and it was as stunning as any Caribbean get- away. She parked her car and began to scramble down the sandy incline, reminded of childhood holidays when she, Myron and Mary-Belle would play beneath the wide beach umbrellas.

The beach should have been deserted but as her canvas shoes sank into the soft sand she looked up and saw a yacht in the water, lazily swinging to her anchor in the gentle breeze. Her expert eye ran approvingly over the boat's beautiful curved lines and even from here she could see the glint of sunlight on varnished wooden decks. Her eyes narrowed, because on the beach a short distance away from the boat stood a man. And not just any man.

She knew straight away it was Rafe. She didn't need to see the broad shoulders or powerful physique or the black hair glinting in the sunlight; it was much more visceral than that. Every pore of her body screamed out to her in shocked and delighted recognition, but she fought back the latter feeling, resisting the desire to kick off her shoes and go running towards him with her arms spread wide.

Because they were over and she didn't know why he was here—appearing in front of her and taunting her like this. Had he constructed some kind of elaborate charade with her brother to be allowed to come here? He must have done. She told herself that the anger which followed this surprising realisation was healthy. That it would help her stay focussed and she needed that. Because they were over. They needed to be over.

So why was he here, making her heart squeeze with pain all over again?

The Sophie of a year ago might have turned away, got back into her car and driven at speed to the palace. Because no matter what Rafe's sudden new influence with her brother was, he would be unable to access the Princess if she refused point-blank to see him. But that would be running away and she was through with that.

So she took off her shoes and began to walk across the silver sand towards him, her heart pounding out a powerful rhythm in her chest as she got closer and closer.

'Hello, Rafe,' she said, when she was near enough for him to hear.

'Hello, Sophie.'

Rafe's breathing was shallow as she stopped right in front of him but she wasn't looking at him. She was staring out to sea as if she preferred to look at the yacht bobbing in the lapping water rather than look at him. 'Whose boat is that?'

'Yours. I bought it for you.'

She turned then and he could see fury spitting from her blue eyes. 'You bought me a *boat*? What's this—the billionaire's equivalent of a bunch of flowers to say you're sorry?'

'In a way. But also because she's the loveliest boat I've ever seen and one I thought a sailor of your calibre might enjoy. I cleared it with your brother—'

'I managed to work that out all by myself and I don't give a damn about my brother,' she hissed from between clenched teeth. 'I want to know what you're doing here. Turning up like this out of the blue—appearing on a private family beach without any warning!'

It was the most difficult question he had ever been asked and Rafe knew that he had to get the answer right or risk everything. He wanted to pull her into his arms and kiss her and let his lips demonstrate just how much he'd missed her. But that would be cheating. Even if she allowed him to kiss her, which—judging by the look on her face—he doubted. She needed to hear his words and he needed to speak them. But even so, a lifetime of conditioning was hard to break. 'I'm here because I miss you,' he said. 'Because I've been a fool. A stubborn, unimaginative fool.'

Angrily, she shook her head. 'I don't have to listen to this…rubbish,' she hissed. 'You made your decision, so stick with it! I'm getting my life back together and I don't need you.'

'Don't you?' he questioned. 'Then you are very lucky, Sophie, because I sure as hell need you. Nothing is the same without you. I have a whole world at my feet. I can go anywhere I want. Manhattan, Poonbarra, even England— but I don't want to go anywhere which doesn't have you.'

'Tough. Go away, Rafe,' she said tiredly. 'And take your meaningless words with you.'

'If that's what you really want, then I will go.' He narrowed his eyes. 'But before I do, I need you to listen to what I have to say. Will you at least do that for me?'

He could sense her struggle as she turned her face away from him to look out at the water again.

'Hurry up, then,' she said abruptly. 'Because I want to go.'

He drew in a deep breath. 'I never really believed in love. I wasn't even sure it existed—'

'I remember,' she interrupted acidly. 'You'd seen it masquerading as *lust*, or *greed*.'

'Yes, I had. I'd seen nothing but chaos in its wake,' he continued. 'And that made me determined to control my own life and destiny. That's why I steered clear of any emotional entanglements and it had always worked just fine. And then I met you.'

'Don't.' He could see her jaw working now. 'Don't tell me things you don't mean.'

'I won't. Because what's in it for me to make this admission, unless to admit that I'm fighting like mad to try to get you back, Sophie? To tell you that you appeal to me on every level which matters? You didn't just break through the glass ceiling of my life—you smashed your way in, without even seeming to try. Somehow you made me confide in you. Made me realise that talking about painful stuff was the only way of letting it go. You gave me your body in the most beautiful way I could have imagined. You made the hard-bitten workers at Poonbarra fall completely under your spell, because despite everything this princess has the common touch. I fought it as hard as I knew how and I'm through with fighting because I love you, Sophie.'

'I don't believe you,' she said.

'You can't choose who you love,' he continued doggedly. 'But if you could, I would still choose you. Even if you tell me you never want to see me again, I will never regret loving you, Sophie. Because somehow you've made me come alive. You've made me experience joy—only the flip-side of that is the pain of missing you.'

He saw in her eyes the gleam of unshed tears, and a sudden unbearable thought occurred to him. Maybe he really *had* blown it with his arrogance and his fear. He felt the raw aching of his heart and then she started to speak.

'All my life I've been put on a pedestal, like some kind of marble statue,' she said. 'And when you made love to me, you made me feel like a real woman. Only then I realised that you've imposed all these rules and guidelines about what I'm allowed to do and what I'm allowed to say. I'm not allowed to love you, but presumably I was going to be allowed to love our children. Only love isn't something you can limit, or siphon off. It's supposed to grow, Rafe. We're supposed to spread as much of it around as we possibly can.'

'Then spread some over me,' he said softly, but still she shook her head.

'What if I'm frigid?' she demanded. 'If that night we had sex at the palace is the way it's going to be from now on?'

'You think that?'

'It's *your* opinion I'm asking, Rafe.'

'I thought you must be uptight about being in the palace and so I decided to back off—to give you the space you needed.'

Her voice trembled. 'I thought you'd gone off me.'

'Gone off you? Are you out of your mind?

We were having a communication breakdown, which wasn't exactly helped by palace protocol.'

He met her gaze and wondered if she could read the longing in his. She still hadn't touched him and he thought there was still some defiance in her attitude.

'I'm going to Paris next month. I'm taking a professional pastry course to capitalise on all the cooking I did at Poonbarra.'

'Then I can come to Paris and work from there.'

'Maybe I want the chance to spread my wings and live on my own for a while.'

'Then I'll wait until you're ready to fly back to me.'

'You're so sure I would?'

'That's a risk I'm prepared to take.'

She looked at him. 'Do you think you have the answer to everything, Rafe Carter?'

'I hope so,' he said, his voice suddenly serious. 'Because I feel like I'm fighting for my life here. All I'm asking for is one more chance, Sophie.

A chance to make it right. A chance to show you just how much you mean to me.'

Her lips pressed in on themselves but he could sense she was softening.

'If you ever, *ever* hurt me—'

'I won't ever hurt you again,' he vowed. 'I will love and cherish you for the rest of my days. Just so long as you...' His words tailed off, but he knew that he had to say them. Because they were equals. Because his love for her was fierce and strong, but that didn't make *him* any less vulnerable. And because there was no shame attached in admitting that to the woman you loved. He swallowed. 'Promise never to hurt me either.'

'Oh, Rafe.' And now the unshed tears were spilling down her face and she brushed them away as she shook her head from side to side. 'I will never do that,' she whispered. 'Never.'

His own eyes were pricking as he framed her face in his hands and a swell of emotion so powerful came over him that the world seemed to tilt on its axis. For a moment there was nothing but stillness as their gazes met.

His voice was full of tenderness. 'Do you want to sail your yacht off into the sunset?'

She smiled as she lifted her face to his. 'It's a long time until sundown. I think I'd rather kiss you instead.'

EPILOGUE

A GHOSTLY WAIL shattered the night calm and Sophie rolled over lazily to curl her naked body comfortably against Rafe.

'That's a curlew,' she murmured sleepily, her breath warm against his chest.

'Congratulations.' He kissed the top of her head. 'Soon you'll be eligible for membership of the Australian Ornithological Society.'

'That's not fair,' she protested. 'I know lots about the indigenous birdlife. I can easily recognise a bowerbird.'

He kissed the tip of her nose. 'Only because their colouring is as blue as your beautiful eyes.'

'Oh, Rafe,' she whispered as she wriggled luxuriously against him. 'I do love you.'

'Well, that's good,' he said steadily, though he

could do nothing about the sudden lump which had risen in his throat. 'Because I love you too.'

He pulled her closer, reflecting on the last three eventful years. It had been an *interesting* road they'd travelled together before Princess Sophie of Isolaverde had finally consented to become his wife. She'd meant what she said about doing a cookery course in Paris, but Rafe had quickly established a branch of Carter Communications in the Eighth Arrondissement and they had set up home nearby.

Sophie had graduated from the famous patisserie school with honours and soon afterwards they had married in the Isolaverdian cathedral in a ceremony which included royalty, magnates and film stars. But the glittering congregation might as well not have existed, because all Rafe had been able to see was his beautiful bride, wearing the ruby and diamond necklace which had belonged to her mother and which he had presented to her the day before their wedding, to the accompaniment of her tear-filled eyes and trembling lips. Rafe had been planning to pay any price to get it back from Prince Luc, but the Mardovian royal had insisted on gifting it to them.

'It is yours,' he'd said gruffly. 'For it was always intended for Sophie.'

But there were no hard feelings between Sophie and the man to whom she had once been betrothed—and Luc and his wife Lisa were both guests at the royal wedding. So was Amber, with Conall. Nick, Molly and Oliver. Chase had defied logic and schedules and somehow managed to get himself there from the depths of the Amazonian rainforest and Gianluca was there, too. Even Bernadette had accepted an invitation and Ambrose surprised them all by spending most of the evening dancing with the Irish housekeeper.

And when Rafe had laughingly enquired whether there was some kind of romantic attachment brewing, Bernadette had silenced him with a stern look. 'There is *not*!' she'd declared. 'Sure and all he wants to talk about is his gout!'

After the wedding, Rafe had asked Sophie where she wanted to live, telling her that they could go anywhere she wanted—but her answer hadn't really surprised him. For although they visited Europe and America from time to time, their main base was in Poonbarra, where the skies were huge and the air was clean. It was the only place she'd ever really felt free, she told him. And he felt the same. It was *their* place, now shared with their firstborn—a beautiful bouncing baby boy they named Myron Ambrose Carter.

But before she'd become pregnant, Sophie had experimented with everything she'd learned in Paris and added a few twists of her own—which was how Princess Pastries had come about. Her second cookbook had just been published to great international acclaim and had become an instant bestseller, with all the profits going to an Isolaverdian children's charity. Despite a lot of pressure from the major networks, Sophie had refused all offers to do her own television show. Why would she want to do anything which took her away from her family? she'd asked Rafe quietly.

Why, indeed?

Rafe stroked the hair which lay so silkily against his skin. Family. And love. It was that simple. He sighed. How could something so simple be this good?

'What time is it?' Sophie murmured, her arms tightening around him.

The dawn had not yet streaked the sky and it would be several hours before the wild and beautiful Australian bush sprang into new life. But for now they had the night and they had each other.

Always.

'Time to kiss me,' he said throatily.

And in the darkness, she raised her face to his.

* * * * *

*If you enjoyed this story,
check out these other great reads from
Sharon Kendrick:*

*DI SIONE'S VIRGIN MISTRESS
CROWNED FOR THE PRINCE'S HEIR
THE BILLIONAIRE'S DEFIANT ACQUISITION
THE SHEIKH'S CHRISTMAS CONQUEST
CLAIMED FOR MAKAROV'S BABY
Available now!*

MILLS & BOON®
Large Print – April 2017

A Di Sione for the Greek's Pleasure
Kate Hewitt

The Prince's Pregnant Mistress
Maisey Yates

The Greek's Christmas Bride
Lynne Graham

The Guardian's Virgin Ward
Caitlin Crews

A Royal Vow of Convenience
Sharon Kendrick

The Desert King's Secret Heir
Annie West

Married for the Sheikh's Duty
Tara Pammi

Winter Wedding for the Prince
Barbara Wallace

Christmas in the Boss's Castle
Scarlet Wilson

Her Festive Doorstep Baby
Kate Hardy

Holiday with the Mystery Italian
Ellie Darkins

MILLS & BOON®
Large Print – May 2017

A Deal for the Di Sione Ring
Jennifer Hayward

The Italian's Pregnant Virgin
Maisey Yates

A Dangerous Taste of Passion
Anne Mather

Bought to Carry His Heir
Jane Porter

Married for the Greek's Convenience
Michelle Smart

Bound by His Desert Diamond
Andie Brock

A Child Claimed by Gold
Rachael Thomas

Her New Year Baby Secret
Jessica Gilmore

Slow Dance with the Best Man
Sophie Pembroke

The Prince's Convenient Proposal
Barbara Hannay

The Tycoon's Reluctant Cinderella
Therese Beharrie

MILLS & BOON®

Why shop at millsandboon.co.uk?

Each year, thousands of romance readers find their perfect read at millsandboon.co.uk. That's because we're passionate about bringing you the very best romantic fiction. Here are some of the advantages of shopping at www.millsandboon.co.uk:

* **Get new books first**—you'll be able to buy your favourite books one month before they hit the shops

* **Get exclusive discounts**—you'll also be able to buy our specially created monthly collections, with up to 50% off the RRP

* **Find your favourite authors**—latest news, interviews and new releases for all your favourite authors and series on our website, plus ideas for what to try next

* **Join in**—once you've bought your favourite books, don't forget to register with us to rate, review and join in the discussions

Visit **www.millsandboon.co.uk**
for all this and more today!

H.W -